Penguin Books

THE DAY WE
CUT THE LAVENDER

Jill Neville was born in Sydney and has
lived in Manly, the Blue Mountains, Paris
and London.

She now works in London as a reviewer
and broadcaster and is a Fellow of the
Royal Society of Literature.

She is married to a scientist and has two
children.

This is her seventh novel.

Books by the same author:

THE DAY WE
CUT THE LAVENDER

Jill Neville

Penguin Books

Penguin Books Australia Ltd
487 Maroondah Highway, PO Box 257
Ringwood, Victoria 3134, Australia
Penguin Books Ltd
Harmondsworth, Middlesex, England
Viking Penguin, A Division of Penguin Books USA Inc.
375 Hudson Street, New York, New York 10014, USA
Penguin Books Canada Limited
10 Alcorn Avenue, Toronto, Ontario, Canada M4V 1E4
Penguin Books (N.Z.) Ltd
182–190 Wairau Road, Auckland 10, New Zealand

First published by Penguin Books Australia, 1995
10 9 8 7 6 5 4 3 2
Copyright © Jill Neville, 1995

Typeset in 13/14.5 Bodoni
by Midland Typesetters Pty Ltd, Maryborough, Victoria
Printed and bound in Australia by Australian Print Group, Maryborough, Victoria

Neville, Jill.
The day we cut the lavender.

ISBN 0 14 024823 4.

I. Title.

A823.3

For Judy

Author's Note

In 1974, in the heady days of Gough Whitlam, I received a grant from the Australia Council and, many years later, another donation came my way. These much appreciated gestures helped me to produce (eventually) *Last Ferry to Manly* and now *The Day We Cut the Lavender*.

I also wish to thank my exemplary editor, Jane Arms, who worked patiently on both novels.

My secret belief – the innermost 'credo' by which I live – is that *although* Life is loathsomely ugly and people are terribly often vile and cruel and base, nevertheless there is something at the back of it all, which if only I were great enough to understand would make everything, *everything*, indescribably beautiful. One just has glimpses, divine warnings – signs. Do you remember the day we cut the lavender?

Katherine Mansfield

ONE

It was still there. Australia. It had been there for hours and hours; scorched and crinkling. She had bisected it once with a fine-nibbed pen and black mapping ink, following the explorers' trails, at that first school in the Blue Mountains.

Soon they would see those mountains from above, their mystery reduced. One of the reasons given for packing her off to boarding school, aged six, was that she had a weak chest; mountain air was supposed to have a beneficial effect on chests. She craned her neck and watched out for the sudden contours. They would be landing very soon and her anxiety was increasing by the minute.

Coming back to Australia to ask Vitek for money was her last card. The one she had kept hidden in her darkest corner for emergencies all these years. She had saved him from drowning in the North Curl Curl pool when he was a skinny adolescent, and she was calling in the debt.

Half his size and even skinnier, she grabbed his flailing arm and they were lifted up on the wave together, higher and higher, till she could see the rusty stain of the dripping tap on the side of the surf club. He would have been washed out around the reef, torn apart by sharks. But they rose on the wave's delirious rip, a sensual experience right from the start. 'Thankyou, thankyou,' he kept saying, embarrassed, as he got his breath back, staggering about in the turquoise shallows, the sunlight filtering in golden waves over his legs (so hairy and foreign) on to the white, ridged sand.

How young they were. He used to go on and on about it.

'Ah, youth,' he murmured, his head on one side, his arms behind his head, a hand shielding those eyes as dark as jazz cellars in the Warsaw he'd so recently come from. 'Youth!'

She smiled vaguely. He was congratulating her as if she'd achieved something grand.

'But you're young too!'

'No. I was born old.'

She put it down to all those *lieder* he liked to listen to, about Time Passing and Blossoms Falling and stuff.

Down in the cove on the tight wet sand she wrote his name, VITEK, dragging her stick as if to brand him in her heart, this piece of Europe, dense and pain-ridden, something she needed to know, something that clashed with Australia's genial barbecue culture.

He would lie on their beach, eyes shielded against the glare, contemplating all that must pass. That haughty youth; legs like a young colt. Once he found a sea-horse and laughed.

When Norah brought her Polish boy home, Mother spoke slowly to him, shouting as if he were deaf. He deferred to the parent. Admired her cut-glass sherry decanter and borrowed a book by Aldous Huxley to have an excuse to come back.

He returned on his bicycle with the book and spoke to her mother as if they were the same age. He waved his hands about and bent towards her urgently. 'Huxley says if we go on putting our sewage in the sea it will be polluted in twenty years' time.'

Mother roared with laughter, gesturing out at the mighty Pacific spurting above the cliff, coiling in the rock pool, indigo at its deepest, turquoise in the shallows. Nobody thought you could run out of anything then.

But Vitek presented her with his precious sea-horse and said that soon they would all be extinct.

When Mother had one of her fits there were no favourites. She blamed all her children – Alexandra, Norah, Rufus – for her boring life, the eczema on her elbows, and ranted on about how it had been better when they had all been away at boarding school. Then she swallowed Bex APC and went to bed. Heat and boredom coagulated into afternoons where the children could think of nothing better to do than sit under wire stretchers poking out fluff caught between crossed wires.

Sometimes Norah would run to the edge of the cliff at North Curl Curl and cry into the huge jet of exploding spray, the pull of watery oblivion below her mixed up somehow with her rising hormones.

Whenever Vitek cycled over, her mother put on earrings and played Chopin sonatas on her piano. She even brought out her ivory cigarette holder and poured sherry into the cut-glass decanter before serving it.

'That nice Polish musician came by,' she said casually at dinner while Dad spooned in the silver-side. 'He accompanies me on the violin.'

'Everyone's mad about him except me,' Alexandra piped up. 'He's hairy, and slimy. I heard him tell Mum he'd like to meet her at dawn with forty horsemen wielding sabres. Yuck.'

Alexandra, first born, never played on the reef

or in the caves with Norah. She liked to sunbathe where the sun flashed unimpeded on the chromium of parked cars and parked bodies, roasting methodically first the front and then the back and even the insides of her elbows. Those were the days before the sun had melanoma in it. When she stood up, the sky darkened.

Sometimes Mother met Vitek for a private conversation about Culture and sent the children off to the beach. Norah found another sea-horse as knobbly as Vitek's body and fed it to a huge sucking anemone that reminded her of her mother's eyes.

Now through the plane window the coastline was unwinding its yellow garland of beaches.

To comply with Australian immigration regulations a member of the crew will be coming through to spray the cabin after landing. Please remain in your seats.

She peered out trying to locate North Curl Curl beach. By the time the plane landed she would have time perhaps to call him at his office.

A few thousand pounds would be nothing for Vitek. He was Chairman of Vic Enterprises now, one of Sydney's big-shots.

TWO

He told her to come straight over. She was to telephone a number and tell the taxi company to charge the cab to him. His voice sounded different. More Australian, of course, more flamboyant. There was money in it.

She sat in the back of the cab and didn't speak to the driver, still locked in her London habits. They stopped outside a skyscraper, its mirror-windows flashing with clouds and crowds. The lift ascended in an eerie silence to the thirty-eighth floor as if a neutron bomb had fallen. Why wasn't she nervous? She was about to beg, but she didn't feel at all embarrassed. Maybe that was because the money was not for herself but for her ill-begotten daughter. Nothing mattered to the broody hen in danger of burning to death but the eggs.

She glanced into the lift mirror and saw a fairly attractive woman, going a bit at the seams, and gave herself a macabre flirtatious smile. If the lift crashed, her feet would squelch through her skull like a contortionist painted by a cubist. Everything would end in a mess.

Inside his suite it was all tycoon flash – chrome and steel and gadget lighting. Through the vast curving window she could see right down into the eye of the harbour, which glimmered between city blocks. A rush of wind clawed off a sheet of plastic from a building site and sent it flying off towards the harbour, flapping its giant plastic wing, a demented angel.

A door opened behind her and Vitek approached over a mist of years, both arms extended, a grin crunching up his eyes so she couldn't read their expression.

'Well, well.' With his arm around her shoulder like a boxer's manager, he led her into his inner area. 'In your honour I sent the boys home early.'

There was something that looked like an original Toulouse-Lautrec on the wall. She approached it with a learned stoop, turning away from him, getting a breather from his scorching presence. People didn't change. Hmm, a Lautrec. What she wanted from him would be his fingernail parings. She would ask him, straight out, in a minute.

'They say if an old flame looks you up after many years she must be after one thing . . . money.' When Vitek said the word 'money' his teeth clenched into a snarl.

She laughed, as the Japanese do, at the naked truth.

He was the first foreigner she had ever known. Through him she'd learnt the intimidating power of pleasure. Unfortunately, the sediment was still in her bloodstream.

She put down her bag. 'People must try to borrow money from you all the time.'

'All the time. I say to them, Look I had to walk through shit to get mine, you do the same.'

He circled her, burly with achievements, one eye amused, the other, with its drooping lid, as if he were looking along the barrel of a shotgun.

'Money equals shit, eh? Long live Sigmund.' How squeaky her voice sounded, the voice of a supplicant.

'Aha. Where would we be without Freud?' He was looking at her now, as if to say, The girl's still got it. Pity about the twitches. She needs a drink or two.

'He's not fashionable any more. Nor is Darwin. Or Marx. They've turned against our old gods.' Words haemorrhaged up, rolling in from the chatterbox world. She accepted a drink without asking what it was, letting him take over, as if the last hundred years since they'd seen each other hadn't happened. He picked up a strand of her hair and tucked it behind her ear. She closed her eyes for a moment.

He moved away and landed with a thump on his chair. 'No one wants big daddy any more. But when things go wrong they still scream for him.' He swivelled back and swung from side to side, like a courting chimp on a branch, eyeing her over the rim of his glass, the reflexes of the tired old flirt. There was still a faint Polish accent. There was still the energy. Only the dreams had gone. And youth, of course. But he knew that would pass. He had counted its days.

He prowled around the penthouse chuckling. 'Norah, little Norah. Remember that hypnotist at the hostel? He could get you to go off into a trance in a few seconds. Pouf! You went off every time he counted down from ten. But me, never. He tried and tried, but I could never lose this bloody consciousness.' He jabbed at his balding forehead with two plump fingers.

The hypnotist at the migrant hostel had claimed to cure bed-wetting and all nervous disorders, like her coughing fits.

When she had lain on Vitek's stretcher and closed her eyes, she'd pretended to go into a trance and bided her time; inhaling with joy the faint ammonia intimacy; jerking up when summoned, announcing she was cured, the tickle in her throat gone; swallowing hard; holding her eyes wide and steady to prove it like a bad liar; feeling the perilous atmosphere of the city for the first time, chancy

9

and lovely as bleached driftwood.

'Oh, I was just being polite, you know. Pretending.'

'Are you going up to the mountains to see your folks?'

'After they moved up there, Mother died, you know. But Dad's still around.'

'I heard.'

'And I'll see Rufus too, of course.'

Vitek relaxed at the name as if in the presence of one of his mates. 'Rufus had his head screwed on. Always did. The other shamuses of the sixties were all soft in the brain. Soft around the edges. But look at him now. Beautiful life. Beautiful wife. Beautiful kids. Beautiful house on the sea. It makes you sick.'

'So you keep in touch?'

He looked down at his papers and flexed his fingers as if he were still the hopeful violinist limbering up. 'He went over to England and made the Poms dance to his tune. He can do no wrong now.'

Rufus, the Utopian. But his shining vision had attracted its dark apocalypse, legions of drug addicts.

Now Rufus lived on a cliff overlooking Palm Beach. To his right, the ocean. To his left, the shining coves of Pittwater. In front, an island or two. Each evening he could stroll out on to the verandah and toast the setting sun, sucking in its reflection inside his glass.

'Mother couldn't bear all that sex, drugs and rock 'n' roll.'

'All that hippie stuff about free love! It seems so innocent now.'

'If there's one thing I don't mind my daughter doing, it's that. It seems so harmless in comparison with other things.'

'Not now with Aids.'

'She hasn't got Aids.' Norah spoke too quickly.

'Why should she, for Gawd's sake. Tell me about her? You got married, I suppose. You were cute. Your big straw hats. Your freckles. They teased hell out of you.'

He was genuinely trying to be nice; their encounter hadn't become dutiful, not yet, anyway.

She always had to wear hats because of her skin. The sun filtered through the straw dappling her flesh with golden scales each time she moved.

'They teased you too. We had that in common.'

He had been teased for being too hairy; for talking in a foreign accent; for wetting the bed at the migrant hostel; waking and screaming about air raids and Nazis, twisted in sheets sopping with urine; wet with war-baby tears, sunk to the lowest water table.

11

'I never married, Vitek.'

'I'm sorry.'

'What a funny old-fashioned thing you are. Of course you got married?'

Was he really frightened that she was going to touch him for a loan? He could always smell her real intent.

'Coupla times. Mistakes. Anyway, marriage was made to last until death do us part when the average mortality rate was thirty-five. Forever isn't so long in that case.'

He roared at his own gags, padded in jocularity, his eyes still and dark as a sack of prunes.

She and Vitek could never have married. That would have been too neat, too boneless. The story would have been over before it began. They were each other's first chocolate in the box; there must be even more delectable ones under the next layer, they thought. They were wrong.

'My wives are well looked after. But nothing is enough. I give them houses, custody, income, anything they want, but they still whinge; still want me to fuck 'em, though. Giant vacuum cleaners. Not content until they've hoovered up my balls.'

She didn't plan it. Her drink shot out of its glass and got him right between the eyes. An ice cube slid slowly down his shirt front.

Through the dripping vodka they stared at each other: the thin woman, the fat man.

'Jesus,' he groaned. 'Another mad woman.'

It wasn't just the money she wanted from him, that was the trouble. It would be easier to ask anyone else for a loan. She walked out of his office into the open lift, dragging her grip, feeling febrile, her desire scrambling, the unkillable crab, across dead ocean floors.

THREE

Sydney was an offered goblet, slowly filling with light. Rio and San Francisco with a dash of lime. There were advantages to jet lag: the dawn rising; smelling the sea over the almost-faded car fumes; the imminence of water, sliding under wharves, lapping between barnacled posts in the eerie light.

The all-night cafes still had a few insomniacs, mostly male, mostly emigrés. Perhaps Vitek still came here sometimes, talked his native tongue, played his dear old violin. Sydney was full of Vics and Georges who reverted among their kind to Viteks and Giovannis. The thin walls of hastily constructed personalities echoed with Italian hill villages, Lebanese slums, central European shtetls, Lipari islands; easy to forget how those places had failed to provide the wherewithal.

A tart leaning against a Kings Cross shopfront slowly slid to the pavement, legs splayed, pantless. Syringes in the gutter sparkled in the first light. The Coca-Cola neon flashed its fading cheer into the new day, and she walked on down the hill of car showrooms towards the grassy bits, edged with hosed marigolds.

In The Garden for the Blind she sat down and closed her eyes, imagining what it would be like – utter and complete blindness; inhaling the thyme and lemon verbena intended to console.

But behind her closed eyelids the Black Room in the London tower-block sprang into savage detail. She saw him again, that thug, naked except for a yellowing string vest, as he tried to block her way. She saw herself push past him to the corner where her daughter whimpered under a pile of filthy bedding (the sewer-rat that was her only daughter) and pull her up and out of there, into the light of day. She was the goddess Demeter who had crawled into Hades to drag her daughter home. But each year Demeter's daughter had gone slithering back into the pit. This wouldn't happen to Sophie, couldn't: she'd locked her up in the best clinic in London. And the most expensive. The trouble was, she couldn't afford it.

The sound of footsteps broke into her fear. No doubt some rapist, excited by the prospect of blindness, the lack of the judgmental gaze. She opened her tired eyes and glared out at whoever was approaching with all the paranoia of women

15

alone in big cities, and an old man walking his dog scuttled off in alarm. She must be one of those new kind of barmy females.

Norah plucked a spring of lavender. It smelt of happier days. She should have taken the money from Vitek and run. But he would surely come and find her. She would only have to wait. There would be the smile, the jokes, the fear. Vitek must know what she had bottled up; the force behind the thrown vodka.

Meanwhile, in case he didn't come good, she would have to ask Dad. If she rushed back now and checked out of the hotel she might be in time for the train.

All the way through the western suburbs she read *The Letters of Katherine Mansfield*. It was the same grey volume that had belonged to Mother; a second edition edited by the author's creepy husband, Middleton Murry, and dedicated to her dear, kind, boring, ministering angel, Ida Baker. Norah savoured each line until all meaning dissolved; somewhere between the lines there were clues to KM's lonely period in the South of France, in December 1915:

Coming home in the evening with driftwood to burn, the lamp on the round table, the jar of wild

16

*flowers on the mantelpiece ... Sitting on the veran-
dah in canvas chairs after supper and smoking and
listening to the idle sea ...*

'Well, I got away from the little buggers this
time. They scare everyone in the street. But they
can't scare me.'

A tiny, determined woman had entered the
coach while she was reading and was sitting opposite her, pink from exertion, neat as an institutional
child with her Peter Pan collar and gloved hands.

'I went up to the fuckers once and said,
Okay, beat me up then, you little shits. Beat up a
lady of sixty. Show the world what great big men
you are. Seven against one little old lady.'

Norah frowned sympathetically but kept her
finger on the page. 'What have they got against you?'

'One day, when they're drunk, they'll say,
This time we'll get the bitch.'

'Why don't you just move?'

'I've never run from anything, not since the
orphanage.'

They ground on through the western suburbs
and the story of this woman's life. The usual stuff
with the bad father at its core who could not provide
a thing, especially not love. At Penrith, when the
woman finished her tale, she hopped off with a
wave and crossed over to the opposite platform.
Then she jumped on the train going back to Sydney.

Well, everybody has their outlets.

Norah turned back to hers:

The air is like silk today and there is a sheen upon the world like the sheen on a bird's wing ...

The sheen on a bird's wing. There were often days up here in the mountains like that. From now on she would watch out for them. She would make KM's eyes part of her own optic nerve.

The stations were getting small, the platforms wet and ferny. A gorge twisted open, revealing a lake of jade, a ridge of virgin bush and, here and there, colonial houses with large, sagging verandahs. Soon the valleys flared open on the western side with pockets of swirling mist, surprise parcels from the dawn.

The mountain moisture dripping down the cutting on either side of the tracks had hardly eroded the rocks in her lifetime.

The train was moving on to the topmost point of the mountains. A money-spider was moving over the pages of her book. Surely a good omen. She just had time to read a few more gems.

I would like to embrace my Father this morning. He would smell of fine clothes with a suspicion of cigar added, eau de cologne, just an atom of camphorated chalk, something of fresh linen and his own particular smell – his 'blood smell' as p'raps Lorenzo used to say ...

18

Norah breathed deeply, savouring the mountain air and the approaching hint of Dad. He thumped out on the verandah, holding a copy of the *Sydney Morning Herald* like a weapon. She hugged the old man, he stood to attention as if receiving a medal. She got a whiff of ageing flesh, with a suspicion of whisky added, toothpaste, just an atom of Palmolive soap, something of unwashed pyjamas, and his own particular smell.

'Good Lord, Norah! Is it Christmas week?'

He looked puzzled, exhausted already, longing to get back to bed. 'Anything wrong? Still got that job at the BBC? You don't want to lose that pension.'

She followed him into the dim interior; the familiar bric-à-brac, the same old piano, still with the missing candelabra.

'When did you get here?'

'Yesterday. I slept in the Cross.'

'You should have let us know.'

They passed through the spectral living room and through the television room into the kitchen. It needed a coat of paint; fresh flowers; a life pulse. There was still the framed joke on the wall: 'I am the boss of this house. I have my wife's permission to say so.' Someone had thrown gravy on it.

'So, you've still got that job, eh?'

'They told me I could take three weeks leave.'

Would he swallow that one? If he knew how cumbersome were the workings of the Beeb, he would choke on it. What she had had to do was lie to her masters, of course; something about a dying father. He wouldn't like that much. Anyway, he was immortal.

'I always go back to bed at this time of the morning with my tea and toast and read the *Herald*,' he warned, stacking his tray.

She hadn't seen him since Mother's death. But he was anxious to follow procedure. Or was he still hurt that she had been bequeathed the house next door. And not him?

Mother had sat outside under the pine so ancient it was almost bent double, and whispered, 'Take this, Norah. It's the deeds to *Lyrebird*, the little house next door. Hide it from your father. I'm leaving it to you in my will. He doesn't know. I've already fixed up Alexandra and Rufus.'

Norah had humoured the old lady. The Will Game is what you play when the Sex Game is over. Another form of power. Even this big house, the old family weekender, had not been left to Dad. It had gone to the eldest child, Alexandra.

'Don't worry, Dad. I'll make myself some coffee.'

'There's some Nescafe. Your sister buys it.'

'Have you been well, Dad?'

'I always have my T-bone steak at lunch in

20

the hotel. They expect me. In the evening I have a raw onion sandwich. I put my health down to the regular consumption of a raw onion daily. At breakfast I always have two slices of toast with honey, as you see.'

'Do you take enough exercise?'

He had put on weight and his pyjama cords were dirty. He looked demoralised. This then is what old age is like. There is no such thing as a happy ending. If you don't want to die, it's the ultimate terror. If you do, it's pure despair.

'I walk twice a day to the village. I have my own corner seat in the pub.'

Not even a long lost daughter jumping out of the sky at the wrong time of the year could alter his routine.

'You were stupid to waste money on a hotel in the Cross. Your sister would have put you up. She's still got that house on the North Shore. Or Rufus.'

'How are they all?' He was walking implacably towards his bedroom door. She followed him up the long dim hall.

'Your sister still rules the roost. Rufus, well, the boy's settled down at last. But my grandchildren always want to borrow money. *Borrow?* Ha ha. Whenever they come to see Grandpa, that's what's on their minds. Even your daughter writes from England, all sweet and gooey, then, in the last paragraph begs me for money; some cock and bull story. Every time she swears it will be the last time. Why does everyone ask me for money?'

'Sophie is going through a bad phase.'

'How long can a bad phase last? She should get a job. Has she learnt typing? During the Depression people had to eat nasturtium leaves. But your mother knew how to type. She had a very good job when I met her. Secretary to an importer of bathroom equipment. She used to sit in an office surrounded by lavatories. She could type like the wind.'

'Dad?'

He paused impatiently at the door of his room, glancing down at his cooling toast. 'Dad, I never wrote home to ask for money. Not once. In all those years. Did I, Dad?'

'We should never have let you go to England. It was your mother's fault.'

Mother had always wanted to travel. Her yearning had been almost palpable. Norah remembered sitting, bored, in the kitchen, while a great rainbow of yearning stretched out from her mother to the universe beyond. But when she had hugged her that final goodbye, standing on the deck of the huge white Orient Line ship, Mother had let out a strange deep guttural sob as if she were giving birth to her a second time. Leaning over the railing, Norah had waved and waved until they'd all dwindled away and the crepe streamers had stretched

22

and snapped, bouncing back on to her body like a hundred cut umbilical cords. She had kept a few streamers for souvenirs, moving them from bed-sitting room to bed-sitting room until they faded completely and the champagne cork from the farewell drink in the poky cabin disintegrated.

Norah took her coffee outside. A flock of parrots flew upward in a gust from the apple tree. The long grass shivered; hens cackled in the coop at the end of the garden. From a dead-looking tree stump tendrils of green uncurled, unstoppable. Just like Dad. Ticking over at candle-power but containing reserves of energy still. It was impatient Mother who died too soon; the one who always got out of cars before they stopped.

Agapanthus bloomed, even on the drive. Sooner or later Dad would be sure to make the joke about Agatha's pants. A signboard lay propped near the chicken coop. It bore the name of the old boarding school, faded by rain and years to shades of beige.

On the distant ridge she could see the pines where the school had once been. Magpies used to dive down and peck the pupils' scalps as they filed dolefully beneath. When the school was burned down by some splendid arsonist, Mother drove over and rescued the sign from the ashes, bringing it back as if it were some appalling family responsibility. Now they would never be able to forget that place. Yet it hadn't been all bad. Early in the morning the western slope was the Milky Way, and she would run all the way around the grounds ankle-deep in silvery mist, frosty stars of dock-weed bursting under her feet. Before bedtime they had to go outside and stand in the fresh air and drink the awful scalded milk. Then she would creep out to the very edge of the chasm, deposit the wrinkly milk-skin under a bush and stare around, precipice-encircled, as the grey-greens transmog-rified with distance into blues: cobalt, indigo, tur-quoise and the deep purple of the most distant place. She'd presumed that must be America.

It was probably this plateau on which she now stood.

'Everyone moans about boarding school, tra-la-la,' Mother had laughed during her first hurried visit. 'But Rufus never complains about his. Now cheer up and give your father a kiss, like Scarlet O'Hara,' she'd said, loving her new freedom, her office job, her long red fingernails that tapped with such impatience to be gone, her merry lunches in town. While Alexandra had eaten her way through the box of chocolates, Norah and Dad had performed a Hollywood kiss for Mother's amusement. Norah had bent over backwards and closed her eyes like Vivien Leigh; Dad had smelt of tobacco and his mahogany office in Sydney.

Each parental visit had been a dazzling honeymoon. Afterwards had come the long Arctic. A pattern she had duly repeated in maturity, one that felt real. Or was it the more primitive routine of her babyhood, the four-hourly feed?

Dad emerged from indoors clutching his transistor against an unironed shirt; he who had taken the salute of regiments.

'Now tell me the news, dear.'

'Sophie is causing me a lot of worry.'

'It's the age. Needs a spanking. We were always very strict with you. You all turned out well.'

'How's Justine? Enjoying the house next door?'

'Just because she's your niece doesn't mean she shouldn't pay the rent on time.'

'It gets paid, but it's just enough for the maintenance, really.'

'Justine went through a bad phase too. You should sell that house. Invest in TV shares.' Dad switched on the radio, which crackled. 'Time for the news. Then I have to go over my accounts. Why don't you go for a walk? You can't snoop around your property while they're away. They've all gone down to Sydney.'

Round the corner came an ancient figure pushing a wheelbarrow. 'You can make yourself useful. Give Andy his morning tea and biscuits. There are ten dollars on the mantelpiece. Put it on the tray under the saucer. No more than three biscuits. Maximum.'

She gave him a mock salute.

When she came outside with the tray, Andy was staking zinnias. He stood up, their garden gnome, one hand pressing the small of his back and began wheedling at once his old refrain: 'Give old Andy a kiss.'

She blew him one. Put the tray on the grass and sprang back as if she'd encountered a funnel web spider.

He lurched forward but couldn't quite grab her. 'I've got a bad back.'

'Oh, I'm sorry, Andy. That must be awful.' She stepped closer but poshed up her tone of voice to keep him at bay.

He pulled up his old shirt (one of Dad's cast-offs). 'Cop a feel.'

Andy's sniggers followed her all the way to the back door. Why did Dad hire him? Not out of charity, that's for sure. He wasn't the type.

Indoors, she beat her way through the clammy shadows until she arrived at the piano, the same one they'd had in North Curl Curl. She had often come home from the beach to find Mother storming over Chopin (the second piano sonata in B flat minor), going full pelt with the pedal, the fires of frustration leaping from her fingers. The piano was her mother. Hard but full of some inscrutable joy.

She leafed through the old sheet music. On one cover a couple embraced under a full moon. She propped it up and tinkered with the yellow keys, peering up at one of the old songs, 'A Kiss in the Dark':

I recall the mad delight
Of a lovely dance.
And a stroll into the night
Trembling with Romance.

The room around her was gloomy; light gave up the struggle of penetrating the walls of pines outside. Dad never lit the fire, fearing to waste wood as if it were bank notes. Mother had always had both fires burning recklessly. They had been opposite in everything.

Now only the crockery in dusty cabinets spoke of her style, her sense of largesse. The porcelain frog. The Dutch figurine. The etching of Warsaw. The portrait of the relatives in oils. Opposites might attract, but after that they should go their different ways. Or their children see-saw forever after, first towards everything their mother represents, then towards their father. Now the house felt dead. Father had shrunk inside it, seldom letting in the light. Even his grandchildren avoided the place.

Nora hurled herself into another song:

May I have the next Romance with you?
Take my heart and let it dance with you

And in its ecstasy every beat implores
Darling just to be faithfully yours.

Her voice quavered, couldn't make the high C.

Dad, walking by the open door, paused in a shaft of light.

'What's wrong, Dad?'

He passed a hand over his face. 'Oh, I just thought, for a moment . . . '

'You thought I was Mum. Singing her song.'

'Well, from the back . . . ' He moved unsteadily out of sight. A few seconds later he called out from the kitchen. 'Who let these damned cats in? Their place is in the garden.'

'But, Dad, it's cold up here.'

He returned to the doorway. 'It's good for them. These cats are over fifteen years old. They've thrived on the outdoor life.'

Norah wasn't the only emotional spartan.

Later that night when Dad was slumped in front of a television variety programme with the one-bar radiator in danger of scorching a trouser leg, his top lip pulled down over his lower lip like a bored child, Norah hunted out Mother's sherry decanter, the one Vitek had admired, and drained it methodically. This was from Mother's grand old childhood home near Sirius Cove; when it clinked against a wine glass, Mother had been Gertrude Lawrence swaying about in a droopy dress about to emit a frothy paradox. Well, what was so wrong with that for a fantasy, if you were stuck in the suburbs, married to a plodder and with a love of long words that alienated the neighbours? So she played the piano and seethed while Alexandra, her eldest, bustled about the house in a tiny apron, little Norah sat under the table murmuring to makebelieve friends, and Rufus gurgled.

Norah sipped the last of Mother's sherry in front of the cold grate of home and reached for the warming presence of Katherine. Tonight KM appeared in the opposite chair in a swirl of silk georgette, cut on the cross and glittering.

Why the hell did you marry that shit Middleton Murry, Katherine? Couldn't you see he was just a baby?

Katherine gave a tubercular cough but did not reply. For some hush-hush gynecological reason, never fully explained in her writings, perhaps to do with an abortion or a miscarriage, she had not been able to have her baby. Though she had dreamed often enough of her elfin child, in a flannel gown with a sweet little tuft of hair.

Norah's Sophie had certainly not been an elfin child. She had snored like billy-o and sucked. There had never been any worry that she would stop breathing in her cot. She was too robust for that. No hint, no forewarning of the frailty to come; no shadow of the bad fairy looming over the cradle.

Why did you have a child without a father, Norah? K's voice was soft, sweet and insidious. Now, it was her turn to ask the unanswerable question.

FOUR

The telephone went on and on, drilling into her cocoon of sleep. Whoever was at the other end of the line was very determined. Dad got there before her, standing at bay, his pyjama cords swaying, his hands quivering. 'Who? What? Speak up.'

He glanced at his hovering daughter, at her wan, white face, with a sudden roguishness. 'Laurel! By Jove, it must be twenty years. No, not to lunch. People are expecting me. Come to afternoon tea.'

He hung up with an air of satisfaction. Old lovers were shares on life's stockmarket; they could suddenly appreciate. 'She said she had something to show me.' He chuckled, and a curious look crossed his face that at first she didn't recognise.

'Who's Laurel? An old flame?'

'Haven't seen Laurel since ... God knows when.'

'Let me iron you a shirt, Dad. Before she comes.'

'Good girl.'

'Wear the blue one,' she said, following him down the hall. Then she recognised the look on his face – lechery – the one associated with dirty jokes, the one Mother had hated.

She went out into the garden and wandered about waiting for the kettle to boil. Being the last half of summer, three thousand feet above sea level, there was a distant sense of apricot afternoons, a pleasant falling away of all things harsh. Some leaves were already auburn, and a heavenly blue hung in the air. Here it was, that light on the world like the sheen on a bird's wing.

Cats appeared from the wild area where the pines squeezed through the palings. In the apple tree the parrots kept watch over ripening fruit like sultans over their child brides. Norah glanced possessively next door towards her legacy – her own little house, *Lyrebird*, half hidden in trees and closer to the edge of the precipice than this much bigger house.

The manager of the Mountain Hotel, who was also a voluntary member of the fire brigade, had suggested it would be wise to burn a fire-break round *Lyrebird*. 'Trees near a house are dangerous,' he had said, one arm swinging, as if to hack.

She had nodded affably, thinking of the lyrebird nest in the depths, the huge magnolia and its interlocking shadows.

'And vines around a house encourage insects.'

His voice had had that kind of practical edge that saved the drain pipes but sank the spirits.

The piercing ring of the telephone had her rushing back inside again. Dad reluctantly handed her the receiver. This time it was Vitek. It was obviously the day for old lovers.

'I sat and thought about what you did for me years ago.'

'What did I do for you?'

'You took me home. You showed me a way in. The hostel was just me wanking in a wet bed; recurring dreams about the tram in Warsaw that got bombed while I was running to catch it. The hypnotist in the room next door tried to expunge the memories. Remember?'

'I remember.' A pause for remembrance. The confused din of time gone by.

'Listen, I have to drive out west to see a vineyard. Why don't I drop in on the way?'

'You're going into wines?'

She hung up, certain now that he would give her the cash, that she wouldn't have to sell *Lyrebird*. If he came up here to the mountains, he'd stay a while. In this setting, when Dad had gone to bed, she'd go down on her knees and beg if she had to.

Dad went to the shop and bought some biscuits. He cleaned his room and changed the sheets on the double bed. After lunch at the pub with cronies, followed by his usual nap, he spent half an hour choosing an oval plate from Mother's china collection. At last he changed into the blue shirt and arranged the biscuits on the plate to his satisfaction. Arrowroot, his favourite, on the outside circle and in the middle Continental Fancies with jam centres, a symbol of revelry.

He panted with concentration, and his trembling hands made the biscuits shoot off the plate. He picked them up, grunting, re-shaped the pattern; and now there was dust on the red jam.

Norah brought out the rest of the tea things, but not Mother's best violet cups.

'Make yourself scarce while Laurel's here. We'll have lots to discuss.'

The sound of a car driving on gravel drew them out on to the verandah. They stood in a reception line: the old colonel in the red beret and his smiling daughter.

A gaunt woman in green and white stripes with a dark green peplum was paying off the driver, fumbling elaborately with her handbag and purse, patches of agitated red showing through her face powder.

'Dalton! This is quite incredible,' she cried through it all, then came up the steps with peplum bouncing. All the features of her face curled upwards as if they were pulled by strings. There was a hint of dark, passionate eyes as she offered Dad a cheek to kiss.

'I can do better than that,' Dad said. 'I'm out of practice.'

Laurel laughed, smoothing down her skirt. Her neck blushed. Then she looked at him, just for a moment, in antique conspiracy.

'This is my daughter, Norah. The youngest. Over from London.'

They were entering the house. They were in Mother's living room. Norah felt it as a sacrilege. The violet teacups rattled in their glass-fronted cabinet as Laurel put down her bags; then she rubbed her goosepimpling arms.

'We should light a fire, Dad.'

'It's summer!'

'But, Dad, this house is chilly. And at this altitude.'

'Let's move into the little room. There's a radiator on in there.'

Trembling with concentration he carried in the plate. Continental Fancies skidded all over the

35

place. Laurel retrieved them from the carpet, brushing each one as delicately as if it were a jewel.

'Give them to me. I'll throw them out,' said Norah.

'No, these will be all right. Your Dad's made such an effort. These were always our favourites. You remembered, Dalton. I'm deeply flattered.'

Dad gazed back into her eyes. The tram re-attached itself to the cable. Sparks flew.

Norah retired to the kitchen. There was always a surface to wipe, a teatowel to straighten. She smiled. Now she knew why the gods stayed young forever.

'Why do you live in England?' Laurel asked over tea. 'It's so grey. And London has no self-confidence any more.'

It was odd how sophisticated ladies went for Dad.

'Norah's got a steady job.'

'Australians revel in England's downfall. It's *schadenfreude*,' Norah said.

'I used to like London. I went there as a girl on the Grand Tour. It was the done thing, back then.' She looked at Norah; her face sagged, giving her an odd nobility. 'But you never returned, except perhaps for Christmas sometimes. That must have hurt your mother very badly.'

Having an affair with Dad must have hurt her very badly too. Norah stood up, dropping

36

another biscuit on the carpet and crunched it under her foot.

'I feel nervous seeing your father after all these years. Perhaps he'll think I've got old and ugly.'

'How many years is it?' Dad asked gruffly.

Laurel looked at him and waited for two beats. 'Eighteen years, five months, and four days.'

Flushing again, she turned to Norah. 'I had a crush on your father. But of course. He was married.'

'So we couldn't do anything about it,' roared Dad.

Laurel looked down, amused, at the biscuits. 'Of course not. Your mother was alive. But I read in the papers that she had died. And, well, I happened to be in these parts so I thought, Hmm, I'll ring Dalton and see if he remembers me.'

She's been planning it like a naval operation, Norah decided. She stood up. 'I'm off to stake up the sweetpeas.'

'Perhaps I could take back a bunch,' Laurel said, plump with appropriation of all things that were Mother's.

Had Dad kept her in town or as a weekend treat by the harbour somewhere? It was easy to imagine Laurel flicking through fashion magazines, drifting through art galleries, waiting for Dad. He would have arrived with that same genial expression he had on Friday nights when he brought home

37

prawns and beer. Benevolent, slightly bloated, with a strong sense of the privilege he was conveying, creating in her own heart a permanent soft spot for the perfidious male.

The garden seemed pallid these days, despite Andy's efforts. Since Mother's death all the colours seemed to have gone. Air letters had arrived in London over the years describing these beds of azaleas, the blooming of the wisteria, the restorations after droughts. She had impatiently skimmed all Mother's herbacious ramblings. Old people seemed to put all their sensuality into gardens.

Norah was loin-deep in sweetpeas, holding staking string in her mouth when Dad called her back indoors. Laurel was waiting for her with an amused but proud look.

'I just wanted to show you these snaps before I go.' She gestured to a spread of photographs on the low table. They were all of Dad – in full colonel's regalia, leading his division in the annual Anzac Day Memorial March through Sydney.

They are arranged in chronological order, from fuzzy black and white shots of her father still in his prime – a brave – to the relentless colour of his old age. As each year follows, he does not always age consecutively. Sometimes, bafflingly, he looks younger than the previous year but, by the recent batch, the shoulders are hunched, the head juts forward like the tortoise he is. In the final shots he is standing up in a jeep giving the thumbs-up to the multitude, looking indestructible in his dark glasses, like a Mafia boss; the leader of the pack.

'There's always some bloody thing that spoils the picture,' Dad said, pointing to a lampost, a postbox, or a spindly city tree, something always in the way of a good clear photo of Dad in majesty.

'That's because I had to hide behind something,' Laurel said. 'I had to hide behind something so he wouldn't see what I was up to.'

'Why?'

'I was a married man,' thundered Dad, startling a cat that had sneaked indoors.

Laurel stared at her handiwork. 'I had to have a record of the lost years. It was always worth the wait. Sometimes for hours in the pouring rain while the First World War vets went by and the bands and the nurses, and God knows what.'

They all stared at this epic proof of Laurel's devotion. Banished from his sight (had there been a showdown with Mother?) she had turned up for eighteen years and waited in all weathers for the interminable Anzac march to unwind its bands and its heroes, to record his moment. Waiting, above all, for this moment.

The clock struck the hour with inappropriate sternness, blasting them from their reverie.

'Oh, Lord, look at the time. I suppose I must

be going.' Laurel reached for her Gucci handbag, waiting for her divine reward.

'You're going nowhere,' said Dad.

The next day they went down to the Mountain Hotel to celebrate.

'I wondered, in my fifties, about getting a face lift. But it went no further than that. Now I've accepted the damage age does. But it was hard . . . '

'Were you ever married?'

'Your father was the one. I'd follow him on the bus, the ferry, the tram. As soon as he got off I'd sneak up and sit on the same seat.' She gave a parched smile as if in remembrance of leaner years. 'I just wanted to feel the warmth of his body.'

'He didn't catch you out?'

'He never did. He was always reading the paper, studying the stocks and shares.' She smiled. 'Your father is not the most perceptive of men.'

So, her love was not the blind sort.

Dad came tottering along the hotel terrace with the first tray. All through the night he and Laurel had made so much noise the timbers literally shivered. Norah trying to sleep, in Mother's old room, her books of philosophy and metaphysics on the side table, buried her head under the pillow.

He deposited the tray full of food and went

40

back for another. He forbade either of them to go anywhere near the bar, although it seemed more fun than the silent terrace. She couldn't understand what Dad saw in the T-bone steak. It was mostly bone, surrounded by tasteless chopped lettuce and dingy roast potatoes, a gesture towards real food perhaps.

'How's that famous brother of yours?' said Laurel. 'I've seen him so many times on the box. He's got your mother's brains and your father's sexiness.'

'I'm going to see Rufus the minute I get back to Sydney.'

'Do you get on with him?'

'I never criticise him. That's my secret.'

Laurel's smiling face fell into her tragedy mask. 'You know, I almost looked you up once, oh, years ago, when I visited London for a few weeks. Your brother was there too at that time. Being famous on television.'

'That would have been interesting.'

'But I still had a spear in my side. About your father. I thought you'd be embarrassed. It can get lonely travelling about on your own. I've had lots of practice. I'm one of the head buyers at David Jones.'

'A successful career, then?'

'A career's not everything.'

'You never had children?'

Laurel stood up, ready to grab the next tray that seemed too heavy for Dad.

'Dalton, we should give a party for Norah.'

'Then the whole family can meet you,' Dad said fondly, pushing a chip slowly into her beautiful mouth. Lewdness at the table. Mother would never have allowed that.

When Laurel went to the powder room, Dad fell into a meditation, forgetting for the moment that he was sitting with his daughter. 'I never knew what real passion was until last night,' he said. 'And I'm in my eighties.'

Norah saw her niece's car go up the drive of the house next door, a flash of canary yellow through the mist. Was Alexandra staying with her? Too bad, she'd have to tackle them both tomorrow.

Straight after breakfast she entered the sacred grounds of her inheritance, her *Lyrebird*. Surprised creatures scampered in a flurry of decoy manoeuvres. And there was the house, shabby, sun-dappled, hers.

Justine answered the door in a wrap, hair tousled, face waxen and shut. 'Heavens!' she managed. 'I heard you were back for a surprise visit. Mum said you must be after something.'

Norah tried not to be annoyed at this sisterly

jibe or to glance proprietorially over her niece's shoulder; but she had a sinking sense of muddle and mounting dereliction within.

'How is Alex?'

'Ah, Mum's her usual madly efficient self. I suppose you two are going to start up your old fights.'

'Are you okay?'

'Why, don't I look it, Auntie?'

'I've woken you too early. It's a long hard drive up here in this weather. Last time I did it my eyes were stuck together all the next day; it was all that peering through the fog.'

'It would be more civilised if you came back a bit later. I'll ring you in a while and let you know.'

Norah wanted to prowl around the garden in the angelic mountain dew, to stand where her mother had decreed, feel her celestial satisfaction. But *Lyrebird* would wait for her. The whole garden seemed to hang suspended in morning light. Up here the world was still dappled. 'Glory be to God . . . ' Industry and bad planning had wiped out dappledness from the world. But not up here. Not yet.

FIVE

She was watching the unripe berries twist on the twigs of the juniper tree when a silver Lamborghini came up the drive. Vitek was at the wheel, smiling under his shades.

Dad was down the steps before her, tapping the window with his cane before Vitek put the hand brake on. 'Park the car down the side or the other cars can't pass.'

Not that he was expecting any other car. Laurel had gone back to Sydney for a bridge tournament. Dad issued this standard order to all visitors.

'One of your boyfriends?' he muttered.

'My first, Vitek.'

'Wasn't that the young man your mother absconded with to the Great Barrier Reef? She played the piano at a hotel to support him.'

Vitek came up the path towards them carrying a crate of wine, a huge bunch of flannel flowers.

And somehow he'd got hold of some boronia. Trust him to have booty.

As she stared at him, he merged with that classic memory of Dad coming home from the War. Dad, under the bottom layer of her heart. Dad coming up the path home after years fighting the Japs. So thin his cheek bones stood out. And such dark skin, yellow under the tan from all the quinine he had taken for the malaria. She watched his heroic approach from the upstairs window. Grass skirts dangled over his arms; parachute silks; and there were carved native boats from New Guinea. Between his teeth he clenched two bone knives, hand-carved. Swinging from his hip was the Japanese Samurai sword. The returning warrior, laden with booty. He ploughed the image into her heart.

'Told you I'd come, honey.'

'On your way out West?'

'You can come with me if you like. A vineyard near Mudgee. I'm going into wines seriously. Speaking of which ...' He lifted his flower-bedecked crate a little higher. 'It's Cabernet Sauvignon, the best.'

'I only drink beer,' Dad called from the verandah edge. 'You can put all that stuff back in your car.'

'We'll drink some. For lunch.' Norah led Vitek past the bristling paternal presence; his sullen malarial gaze.

45

'I'm going to the hotel. Will you be gone when I'm back?' Dad called out hopefully.

She rolled her eyes disloyally. 'He's staying as long as he likes, Dad. He's a friend.' Well, more than a friend.

Here he was, fat, balding, opening the crate in her mother's kitchen.

'Dad thinks you ran off to Hayman Island with Mother. He gets things mixed up. But she did go to the Reef and I often imagine her playing the old dance tunes in some beach joint up there . . .'

'Smoke Gets In Your Eyes, These Foolish Things, Begin the Beguine, Thanks for the Memory, As Time Goes By, A Kiss in the Dark and let us not forget her favourite, May I Have the Next Romance With You?'

'Jesus, you remember her repertoire.'

The cork came off with a pop, and Vitek gave her an amused look. 'She always played those numbers at Hayman Island.'

After that bombshell Norah sat down, staring at the boronia and flannel flowers, yet to be arranged. How the hell had he got hold of them? Money could buy you anything, even protected flowers.

Vitek took over the job of host, choosing the glasses, pouring the wine. He let her stew as he sang.

What is my fate? I await your answer

46

So tell me what will it be,
You're my destiny – may I have
The next romance with you?

He sat down and picked up Norah's cold hand. 'Every morning she would get up before dawn so she could go down to the beach and turn over the turtles that the fishermen had left lined up on their backs on the shore so they wouldn't waddle down to the sea and swim away. Your mother rescued them all. She saw them lying there, crying turtle tears and she turned them over, one by one, so that they all escaped by dawn. We were hounded out of the island in the end.'

'My poor father, giving up Laurel. He could have started a second family. Punched a hole in our sad little routines.'

'Your mother was always so discreet. We used to have our assignations in the hut on the cliff. She was still quite attractive, you know. And there was not much romance in her life. They're such little work, older women. You don't have to woo them or listen to their bullshit for hours.'

'That was after I rushed off to London, I suppose.'

'Before, Norah. It started the very day you brought me home, when I borrowed her Aldous Huxley. She had such a wonderful library for those days, especially in the suburbs. She came outside and put it in my bike basket. She touched my hand

47

for longer than was strictly necessary. I got the message.'

'What about me?'

'You were a child.'

'Child!' She forced herself to look at this thuggish presence in her mother's old house. His well-cut suit and expensive shirt. There was a solidity to him, a man at home with power, a factory for sperm.

Dad lumbered into view, holding his walking stick, ready for his inflexible pub lunch. 'Put those bottles somewhere safe, or you'll have an accident. Haven't I met you somewhere before?'

'I don't think so.'

'Didn't Norah bring you home from the beach? Or were you something to do with my wife's social work?'

'Norah and I were playmates.'

Dad's expression modified. 'Try to stay until sunset. Norah will take you for a walk to Pulpit Rock. You can't go away without seeing the view from there. It's so beautiful it cures the blind.'

Norah started. Usually her father talked in clichés, ran on tram lines, never dabbled in fancy imagery. But now and then he would come out with an oddity like that. Was it something he'd been saving up, to trundle out in an emergency?

They had lunch on the lawn. The sheets she had washed that morning flapped in the sun. The air was delicious with wood-smoke drifting

48

up from the caves. Picnickers must be making barbecues down where ridges and jutting edges of the valley's fall gave refuge to the remaining wildlife and where climbers sometimes ventured, hunting for caves and waterfalls. Once she had seen surveyors down there, trying to measure the immeasurable.

'I'm sorry I shocked you about your saintly mother.' Vitek looked amused.

'I've lost confidence in my judgment. If we mentioned sex, she said we had minds like sewers.'

'Oh, we were all right, because it was romantic. That little hut on the headland, the pounding sea below. Remember that great spurt of spray? It was extraordinary. You couldn't see the hut for boronia. All gone now, of course. I had to camouflage my bike with the stuff when I parked it outside. There was no furniture. Just a mattress on the floor and an old-fashioned safe on a rickety table. Each leg of the table stood in a saucer of water full of drowned ants.'

She remembered. Once she and Rufus had raided it, by loosening the fly screens. There'd been a plate of rotting fruit; the safe on the rickety table; the drowned ants. They had taken home some raffia table mats. Trophies for Mother.

But that had brought on her most memorable tirade. 'You mean you stole these things?' she had screamed. 'You broke off the fly screens and barged in there. That's a criminal act. I've always suspected criminal blood on your father's side. Your father's only hour of glory was in the army. And he liked that because it's mostly ordering people about and giving him the chance to kill things. If I ever catch you kids stealing again, even so much as a pen nib, you're going straight back to boarding school. Now, get out!' By the time she had finished even the air had eczema.

'Your mother was lovely to me. I stopped wetting the bed.'

'So we were all in love with you.'

'Not your sister.'

'You're not Alex's thing. She likes the open air type.'

'I was a slimy continental.'

'Now I understand why she was so keen on getting rid of me, sending me as far away as possible, to the other side of the world. She was getting me out of Mother's way.'

'Perhaps she just wanted to get you out of her way, period.'

Rage leaped like kerosene flames. Norah clapped a hand to her face as if to quell an explosion, ran out of the room and locked herself in the chilly bathroom.

He called his farewells through the door. 'I'm getting bored with your tantrums. You're just like your mother.'

Lyrebird was all sealed up again. The shutters were closed. The gate padlocked. Nobody answered the phone. The garage was shut tight.

'You can't snoop about when they're away. Anyway, what's the rush?' Dad said, giving her his empty tray to clean the next morning, drawing her into a new routine.

'I haven't got a lot of time, Dad.'

Once they switched on the television and caught Rufus interviewing paedophiles.

'Paedophiles! Are they the swine who interfere with children?'

'Yes, Dad.'

'Kill the lot of them.'

There was a sound liberal argument against it. But damn all that, every parent knew that one uncontaminated childhood was worth the lives of a thousand paedophiles. If anyone had tried to hurt Sophie, she would have splattered him against the wall, wound his intestines around the nearest tree.

But Sophie had been damaged. And some man had encouraged the process. Had she torn him apart? He had stood there trying to stare her down in the Black Room, flexing his muscles in his yellowing string-vest, and she had walked straight past him.

Norah escaped into the living room and sat under the dim reading lamp. She would read her book. Her book of books.

In Bandol, in the South of France, where KM had stayed at the beginning of the war, thinking the sea air would be good for her, she'd strolled along the beach one evening, but had been pestered by a soldier and returned to the hotel. An Englishman had knocked on her door. He was the head of Guy's dental hospital in London.

Such a heavenly day today. There seems to be a ring of light round everything; it's still and sunny. So still you could hear a spider spin ... And that Englishman, terribly shy, knocked at my door. It appears he has a most marvellous cure for just my kind of rheumatism. Would I try it? I never saw a man so shy. I can't think what frightened him so.

Norah smiled. She thought she knew what frightened him so, this dentist, so manly in the old way, a younger replica of K's father in New Zealand, her beloved pa-man.

The dentist was married for sure. But Aphrodite, the goddess of anarchy, did her usual business. Norah could see the ring of light around K and her beloved dentist, glowing there, between the lines.

K would have loved Dad; he was a real pa-man too. She wouldn't have belittled him, like Mother used to.

Norah felt that old heave of anger, hating the purple lipstick on her mother's teeth when she gave her big false bright smiles, but forcing the anger back down, as usual.

Norah ignored Dad's instructions and climbed the fence into *Lyrebird*. With every footstep she disturbed some scuttling creature as she circled her dilapidated house, no doubt brooding about the guttering, the cesspit, the tank-filter, the rotting shed. An estate agent had assured her that the property would bring a lot of money now that the motorway was going to be extended. Victorian timber hideaways like these were becoming fashionable. But she grieved at the thought of having to sell it. After all the bad tempers and screaming fits *Lyrebird* had come as a wonderful surprise, her mother's great gift. That and Life.

For a long time she sat on the white rock, listening to the approach of night, transfixed by the rising moon. A dingo howled somewhere down in the valley.

Ah, how nice if KM and she were really twin souls. They had both left the colonies eager-hearted on huge white ships, felt the umbilical snap of the streamers, and suffered genteel poverty in Chelsea. Outsiders. They had even shared the same bedsitting room over a canal in Maida Vale, although Norah didn't find this out for many years. They had lain awake, coughing their hearts out, staring up at those same plaster rosettes on the ceiling, no doubt brooding about sex, feeling the stab of homesickness ...

A preposterous coincidence had kicked off her Mansfield obsession. An old woman from New Zealand tottering about London on her valedictory Overseas Tour had met Norah at a friend's house. From her capacious handbag she had drawn out two letters, both decorated with charming sketches. Many years ago the old lady had received them from her bosom friend Katherine Mansfield, who had later became so famous. There had been a huge bundle of them (KM had a schoolgirl crush on her), but the rest were burned by mistake by some silly housemaid doing the spring-cleaning. *You want them, Norah? Take them. They're yours.* She had slid the tempting letters across the polished table. After a serious inward struggle, Norah had nobly refused the gift. It would have been like taking her diamond rings. The old duck must have been ga-ga, or so damn lonely she had to bribe people for company.

Weeks later a gift arrived from New Zealand, a carefully knotted, brown paper parcel. When she unwrapped it, there, nestling in white tissue paper lay a pale blue bed-jacket threaded with matching blue ribbon. On the attached post-card the old lady had written that many years ago she had knitted the same feather-stitch pattern in the same colour for Katherine, before she went off to London. It was extraordinary how much Norah had reminded her of dear, impulsive Katherine.

Sometimes, on grey, lonely winter mornings Norah would tenderly unwrap K's bed-jacket and drape it over her shoulders, then go back to bed and stare out at the grey, lonely London sky.

Would K have fancied Vitek? Or would she have seen him as fat and corrupt, a fixer? She had a piercing eye.

The dingo howled again. A lonely sound. She remembered it from boarding school. There had been a pack of them down in the valley, then. If it was a portent, let it be a good one.

After dinner Dad took out a battered card-board box and sorted out his old cheque stubs, ruminating over ancient transactions, those anguished times when he had been obliged to part with money. He gazed at each stub as if it were the stump of a severed limb. It would be impossible to ask him for a loan, even for the rest of her legacy, in advance. Worse than lighting all the laid fires in the house at once. Like extracting his bone marrow.

If an explanation was needed, she only had to recall what she'd heard of Dad's father who had been such a profligate. A gambler and a shit, despite his posh English accent. So prodigal he was banned from the Randwick Race Course.

Dad was up to the year 1932 when the door bell rang. It was Vitek standing there, one arm resting on the lintel. A sunburnt Vitek.

'Come on in . . . we'll open some of your Cabernet.' Her face was flushing.

Dad stood up. 'This is inconvenient. I have affairs to attend to.'

'We'll go into the next room, Dad. Come on, Vitek.'

In the sitting room, clammy with disuse, she asked Vitek for a match and lit the dusty kindling that had been laid since Mother's funeral. The room burst into violent life, pine cones popping like fireworks. That brought Dad in.

'You've lit the fire,' he said, peering at the blaze with disapproval.

'That's right.'

'It's a waste.' The unbridled flames seemed to him something that should be quelled, like undisciplined troops. But he was beaten by the mutiny.

'I'll lay another one tomorrow morning.'

He left the room, his shoulders high with disapproval. She placed the vase of boronia on the table between them. Boronia always reminded her of Mother.

'I'm thinking of selling my house, the little one next door, set back in the trees.'

'It's not a good time to sell.'

'I need the money.'

'It's a pity to sell your slice of Australia. You'll get sick of Europe one day, when the fumes cover the land, and there's no difference between all those pungent little countries; when there's not an inch of countryside left to ramble in without a fucking Rambler's Pass.'

'You've got your developers here too. And nuclear waste.'

'Radiation will never reach this altitude. You'll be the survivors. You'll start a new civilisation.'

'How's business? How come you're so successful? In league with the Mafia?'

He gave her his gangster grin. 'I see nothing, I hear nothing; that way I live to be a hundred.'

'How long did your affair with Mother last?'

'Young men with old mistresses seem to need young girls too, for their egos.'

'It was a bit incestuous though, wasn't it, me and Mum? I'm amazed you didn't try my sister. And brother.'

'Why are you so aggressive? You never used to be like this. Never had kids?'

'Aha, you believe in the screaming womb syndrome. As a matter of fact, Vitek, my womb has already done its stuff. I told you before. Remember? I even wrote to you when she was born, many years ago.'

'Did you?'

'Why are you playing dumb?'

'I forget things. Brain cells dying off. What's she like, this kid of yours?'

'She's got your cheekbones. She's just like the poster you had on your wall at the hostel. The little Polish peasant girl on the swing with one foot pressed into the arch of the other for comfort. That little girl, she entered my womb. I lay on my back beneath you so often, staring up at her pretty face, I re-created her.'

'Je-sus.' He screwed up his eyes and looked at her as if she was floating away on a distant raft. 'You're telling me she is my daughter? Is that your game?'

Norah stared hard at the boronia. 'Sophie is your daughter, certainly.'

'What's her surname?'

'Same as mine. Of course.'

'Mine. Mine. Mine. You mothers, you'd like to swallow your cubs whole.'

Dad flung open the door. He was standing in a combat crouch, his red beret at a military angle. They stared at him while he got down his

Samurai sword from the wall, released the secret catch and slid it out from its scabbard. It shone menacingly through layers of grease. With one arm extended, he wielded it above his head like the Lord High Executioner, then swung it down with a 'Hah,' very Japanese sounding.

Vitek flinched and Dad grinned.

'Just feel that blade.'

Vitek touched it gingerly.

'The Japs didn't muck about.'

'I suppose you had to kill the officer, sir, before you could take his sword.'

'Could be,' Dad said, obscurely triumphant, easing the weapon back into its embossed sheath. 'But in this case the officer gave it to me. He was ashamed because I had prevented his death. he wanted to die, of course, like a good little Jap.'

With a grunt he hung the sword back on the wall and sat down, staring scathingly at the leaping flames. 'We'd been dealing with war crimes for days. Three officers had to agree on the verdict, then the accused was shot. This particular Jap was accused of cannibalism. The other two agreed that he was guilty. He had eaten human flesh.'

What a pantomime. Norah noticed that Vitek was getting interested. The war baby liked war stories.

'All the Jap had done was find the corpse, you see. He didn't kill it first. I told them I'd have done the same thing myself. So they couldn't shoot him. I'll never forget the look of loathing on his face. The opposite of gratitude.'

'It's not exactly cannibalism if the flesh was already dead,' Vitek said. 'There should be another word for it. Were you there when the Japs signed the surrender in the Pacific?'

'I'll show you my album.'

He left the room. Norah's face lost its soft expectancy. She had just tracked down the father of her child and he was going to spend all evening looking at war souvenirs of the man he had cuckolded. She knew Dad's sword play was only half fooling. He would like to see Vitek's head on the carpet and ditto with all junior males in the herd.

'We'll never have a chance to talk things over. He'll stick here until dawn.'

'Pity.' Vitek looked straight at her, into her, a fully focused look, his face stilled by the flames.

'Perhaps we could meet for lunch in Sydney and talk?' Her voice came out trembling.

'Is it money you want, my girl?'

'Certainly not.' She sat up sharply. She didn't want it to start like that – it would warp their future together. First he had to warm to the idea of Sophie, and then pay the overdue maintenance. The emotional bill would not be so easily settled, she knew. Sophie had a hollow where a father should be. Girls with loving fathers as well as loving

60

mothers had an indestructible confidence. One-parent families were a bad idea, a shallow fashion. The children had no one to turn to when the single parent failed. They were birds trying to fly on one wing. Everyone now knew they needed dads; boys for a role model; girls for their approval. Cosy mothers – it was most unfair – were less rarified coinage. It had to be a man their mother couldn't banish on a whim. Her forever and forever father on earth, her tree-stump that would always give out leaves.

'But you could acknowledge your daughter's existence, you could write to her.'

Vitek moved uneasily in his chair. He had other children. They would be jealous of the intruder, another pretender to the throne. He twisted his token wedding ring. 'I'll look her up when I go to London in the summer.'

'I told her you were dead. It explained your silence.'

'I remember now. You promised to write to me care of your house at Curl Curl because the migrant hostel was full of kleptomaniacs. I remember trekking over to Curl Curl after you went away. There were air letters for everyone else, but never one for me.'

'I wrote. I wrote. When I didn't receive a reply, I thought, Oh, well, he feels blackmailed, trapped.'

'I thought you had an abortion in London. I thought that's why you went there. To get rid of it.'

'I was going to. But something stopped me. I wonder who destroyed all my letters to you, Vitek?'

He looked down at his hands, as if he were regarding their messy past with the detached air of the grandmother in the portrait above them contemplating the bizarre future she had helped bring into being.

Somehow it didn't seem to matter much any more.

In the morning she tackled her father between the kitchen and the bedroom.

'It was half past ten. You ordered him out. As soon as you finished the entire history of the Australian Infantry in the Pacific. You didn't even ask him about his war experiences. His parents were killed in Warsaw. You could've let him stay the night. It's a lousy, dangerous drive down all those hairpin bends to Sydney in the fog. You pushed him out at ten bloody thirty.'

He edged past her. 'I'm not letting a foreigner hang around all night with my daughter in the same house.'

She stared at him incredulously. The house

had rattled all night from his own lust. Was he still guarding her phantom virginity?

'Dad, I've been around the world on my own. I'm several decades over the age of consent.'

'Won't have these young pups hanging round, using my place as a hotel,' he muttered, retreating with his tray, his emblematic toast and honey, the daily drill against senility.

SIX

The restaurant on the beach had been taken over by Vic Enterprises and filled with plants and pinkish lights; even the windows were pink. It was more casual than the rest of the chain to make allowances for the sand blowing in and the reckless beach spirit.

'Try the yabbies in seaweed. Fresh this morning or I fire the chef.'

For a long time happiness had become something very tiny and far away: a postcard of a Bonnard on a mantelpiece; a snatch of Mozart on a car radio; an encounter in the street with an intelligent cat. These represented a state she had once known casually and accepted as her element. Now raw happiness slapped at the window, like the sea wind. Her body for so long just a sack of innards that for some reason she had to cart around everywhere had become the waves rising to form Venus.

He buttered his roll, giving a magisterial nod to the hovering waiter. 'I hire lots of Poles. They can do anything. Electricity. Plumbing. Building. Anything. But cooks they're not. I have a German cook, a big blond Aryan.'

'You're more forgiving than Dad. He would never, for instance, hire a Japanese gardener. Our gardener is nuts; can't garden, but he's an old Anzac.'

'Those old-timers. Come to think of it, we're old-timers now. So we'd better not waste a minute. When have you got to go back to London?'

'If I'm not back next week, there'll be someone else sitting at my desk. I'm one of the readers. We're bombarded with radio plays. They all go straight into the slush pile. Guess who's got the job of sorting them through? It's like sieving shit. Now and then a bit of gold glints up at me and then it gets exciting.'

This twitchy woman opposite him, disemboweling her bread roll with her definitely ungainly hands, what connection was there between her and the affable child in the straw hat who had once scrambled round the rocks with such native agility? She had clung to him in the hostel for New Australians, wrapping her bony legs around him. She had brought a shopping bag of groceries – charged no doubt, to her mother's account at the general store in Curl Curl.

Later they did it a lot, mostly on her verandah when her parents went out, her mother giving Vitek glowing looks when they returned, never suspicious of her own pubescent daughter, despite the blatant hormonal shine on her face.

The problem with the hostel had always been the sheets. When he tried to dry them in front of the fire, the ammonia pong was overwhelming. He had believed he would never be able to spend a whole night with a woman because of the shame of it. Luckily Norah had always had to get home before midnight.

'Before I catch the plane, Vitek, I've got to put my house on the market. I meant to show it to you when you came up, but ...' They smiled in unison. Dad had cut short that fatal visit with his Samurai sword. '... it's a lovely old place, hidden among the magnolias at the back there. I really will have to sell it ...'

Please God, she wouldn't really have to. She could always ask her brother. Maybe Rufus would be in the money. He was generous, but for that reason he was usually skidding along on an overdraft. Maybe, just this once, as well as the Fame and the Girl he would also have the Money.

Vitek contemplated Norah. There were morbid shadows in those eyes that had once been so sparkling. Something had hurt her beyond her

66

capacity. Well, he knew what that was like, read the signs.

'How will you get your money over without losing most of it in tax and bank costs? Maybe I can help you.'

Financial racketeering. She tried to concentrate on what he was saying, but after a while imaginary love-bites of just the right pressure went up and down her body. Being in a state of desire was like coping with a team of riotous red setters. He was saying something about the money-market; when he looked up and saw her staring at him, her bread roll all in pieces, her pupils shamelessly dilated, she felt herself blush.

The resentment from all those years of neglect had dropped away leaving the beast within perfectly refreshed.

'Is she pretty, my little bastard?'

'Oh, lethally. You know the power of a pretty face.'

He reached over and touched her hand. 'Takes after her Mum.'

'No she doesn't.'

'Why don't you bring her out to see me?'

She stared down at a worm of seaweed. 'She's a heroin addict, our daughter. She's in a clinic.'

He released her hand. Now he understood the shadows, the desiccated bread roll. 'God, Norah, I'm so sorry.'

All the fun went out of his face, and for the first time Norah noticed he had jowls.

'It's an unlucky generation. Pollution. Holes in the ozone. A tired old world losing its shine. I blame the media gurus. Timothy Leary. William Burroughs. Your charming impresario brother. It was cool. It was trendy. You were a sissy if you didn't put your head in the fire.'

The waiter came and took the plates. He recommended the John Dory and told today's joke: 'You know about the two Jews who went up to heaven?'

They laughed politely, but Vitek was looking at his watch. Misery. When the waiter stopped pestering them, he said, 'It's the Third World War. The cannons may be silent, but the human fodder gets devoured as before. My marketing manager, his son jumped off Santa Monica pier. A pupil of Leary's. High on LSD. The whole family emigrated to Australia. They had the idea it was pure here, unsullied. Maybe it is in Iceland. I hear they still don't have Aids on the North Pole. Maybe it's all that snow. But it won't be immune for long. It's the Fifth Horse of the Apocalypse, and it'll wreak its havoc there as well.'

A seagull skidded against the window, but neither of them looked up.

'I used to blame it on TV. I let her watch

too much. Maybe she got stuck on the instant fix.'

'Boredom is the mother of invention, eh? It was boredom that spurred me on to make a one-stringed violin (my first). It was raining I remember; a boring Warsaw drizzle.'

'All TV sets should be lined up against the wall and shot,' she said attempting a smile.

'You lionesses who have lost your cubs are dangerous beasts.'

She told him about Sophie: the hopeful school days; the musical talent; the switch to singing in night clubs, as decadent as the Weimar Republic; her writhing body scissored with laser beams; her delicate voice largely unheard in the fray; she left out the cheating, shop-lifting, stealing, and the endless lies.

'Her gimmick was that she played the violin as she sang.'

Vitek stood up. He had to make a phone call. But he'd like her to come with him afterwards while he said hello to the kitchen staff.

She went airily through the routine, trying not to communicate her disappointment. She had been dismal company. He would never come to visit them in London in the English summer. He would send the odd Christmas card; leave a small legacy in his will, when it would all be too late.

69

'The yabbies were overcooked, Carl.' Vitek was speaking to the cook, his hand on the shoulder of a blond giant in a chef's hat who held a chopper in his huge hand. Dismantled chickens were scattered on the wooden board. The rest of the kitchen blazed with high-tech efficiency, shining with cleanliness down to the tiniest chopping knife. At the far end of the room, standing in a mess of lemon rinds and bread crumbs was the human factor, a small, crumpled figure stirring a vat of something. As she approached him, smiling, she saw the churning taramasalata.

'Pete!'

He turned off the whisk. 'Hello, Norah. Come home for good this time? Yer Mum'll be pleased.'

Mother had met him during the days when she did charity work and used to give him odd jobs. His eyes were still as sad as a donkey's, but if you didn't look too closely he could have been a racecourse tout; he had that same stunted energy.

'Mum died a couple of years ago.'

'She was all right, your Mum. I was only thinking about her the other day, how she collected all them shells for the incurables in the hospital so's they could make boxes and necklaces. She took it hard, you not writing home for weeks on end.'

Wearily he bent down and put refuse in the bin. 'Will we be seeing you in here again? Mr Vic comes in often with the ladies.'

She examined his electric whisk closely. 'I'm going back to the mountains. Dad lives there now. He sold the Sydney house.'

'Whereabouts in the mountains?'

'At the very top. Nice views up there. Like a Raj hill station. But nothing much goes on.'

Pete looked furtively at the approaching boss and took back the whisk.

'Don't be surprised if you see me up there some day,' Pete shouted over the whirring noise. 'You never know. Can't stay in this dead-end job. The pay's ratshit.'

Vitek took her by the elbow, steering her away from the staff, and called back to Pete. 'You can always swim outside. Not many jobs offer you that.'

'Too many sharks out there, mate.'

Vitek paused, lifted a lid from a simmering pan, and scanned the machinery. 'All right. Let's go, Norah. Would you like a lift back to town?'

In his Lamborghini, the corpulent Mr Vic smelled like skinny Vitek. She would have known that smell in hell. Unchanged, feral, irresistible. Bottled and sprayed over cinema seats there would be a stampede of women. Visually he would not

71

turn heads any more. But the power was more alluring.

'Who's Pete?'

'An odd-job man Mum used to hire. Married a woman who already had four children. She forced him to have a vasectomy. Then she upped and left him.'

'Bit of a loser, eh?'

Men driving expensive cars. Being in the front seat next to them. Watching them move the gears. Your body was the car. The gears, the wheel, the indicators your erogenous zones; your flesh under their hands. Speed the lust. All somehow reprehensible: machines, manipulation, the fish-eye of the lecher; that bit of the brain lobe where we all tear at each other's flesh. Bikes weren't like that. Vitek on his rusty bike. That had been romantic. Full of fresh air and youthful aspiration.

'Let's go to the office and fuck.'

A sigh exploded from her. She reached out and touched the back of his neck. It was the smell that did it. Still, it wasn't as if she were a virgin maid, heart full of Beethoven and majestic plans for her future. She had no right to expect romance.

Going up in the lift to his office suite, he nodded once or twice to his staff. She noticed a cringe in the eyes of those he glanced at, an over-anxiety to please. Maybe she had it too.

What would he say to his secretary? When

they entered the top floor, her annex was empty. Vitek had gone off to phone after the lunch. Had he told the secretary to make herself scarce? Was this the boss's post-prandial liqueur? He took lots of ladies to the restaurant, Pete had said, with magnificent tactlessness.

She asked about the Lautrec lithographs, peering at the master's signature. But he was drawing the huge white curtains so she couldn't see them clearly. 'I'm prettier in the dark,' he joked, starting to undress. 'I've got a little fatter since you picked me up in the pool.

'I'd like to do it on the desk,' he said. 'When I'm bored with my afternoon appointments, the thought of it cheers me up. I doodle on the blotting paper, pretending I'm listening, remembering what was on that paper earlier in the day. Come here!'

She stepped out of a pool of summer cotton, still wearing her high-heeled sandals. The decadent touch. This new Vitek would like that. This motherfucker.

'Now lie down there!'

The light edged sufficiently through the curtain slits to enhance this archaic act in the tower block.

'A nice body,' he said, 'ripe, but still taut. You women are best just before you start to go off.'

He might have been talking about the yabbies.

He did everything right. At first her glance flitted about the room, but after being primed up her eyes became slow, huge, absorbed. She could look at him unselfconsciously, his heavy, twisted face, while the burning region inside her swallowed his penis with ferocious joy, a fed anemone. After all these years, after all the sorrow, it still worked between them. Nobody changes, not in their sexual soul.

The delicious orgasm made the desk wet. That should get him through a tedious afternoon. Her deeper orgasms came only in dreams. They were too connected with absolute trust for real life. That sort of trust had shattered like a dropped mirror when she was left, so young, in that horrible boarding school, nature her consolation prize.

'I'd like to spank you. Women like it. Especially the bossy, independent ones. But it's too late now. I can't do it again for hours. Isn't it pathetic?' He was busily dressing. His voice friendly but patronising, like it was in the lift. The earth hadn't moved. Not for him. Nor had the solid teak desk.

She sat up, flushed. Feeling well oiled but just slightly ashamed. Christ, even the lyrebird in his grove does a mating dance more subtle than a lunch at the Vic Restaurant.

Once he had desired her, by the waters of the pool.

He gave her a brandy, patted her bum.

'Come and see me before you disappear for another hundred years.'

He was dying for her to go. Dying to throw her out of the window. But there had been a moment there, on the desk, when he cried out, and she was back in the hostel again for the last time, on that sheetless bed, under the poster of the peasant girl on the blossom-entwined swing, the room smelling of urine and love.

SEVEN

People were streaming into Wynyard Station and queuing for buses to the Quay. The sun was still high enough for a swim. Dad used to come straight home from the office and have his dip. And he always had that early morning swim. When she was little, he used to put her on his back and swim out to the shark-net, head dipping in and out of the sea, face contorted in foam, brown arms ploughing onwards. She clung on tight, trying not to strangle him or bounce off his slippery wet back straight into the jaws of a shark.

He had never let them down. Even when Mother's tantrums tore up the sky. Who was she to criticise him now, send up his savage routines?

A cinema complex advertised a festival of vampire films: bald vampires, comic vampires, debonair vampires, vampires with bloody fangs, and of course Count Dracula. How Sophie had loved Dracula. She was the nubile young girl tossing in her virgin bed while the Count waited outside under a magnetic moon in his long billowing cloak. In the end she went to him, of course.

Tanned women walked by in greens, pinks, yellows. Colours that would be unflattering against a dingy London skin. Vitek must have been embarrassed by her dowdiness. He would be used to these brown, audacious women in bangles. She had come from a paler tradition: mostly Anglo-Saxon and Celt, with maybe a whiff of Jewish. There was that yarn about a grandfather having been the black sheep of a noble English house. Probably the usual bullshit. You could lie as much as you liked about the Old Country because there was no one to catch you out in those days.

She paused in front of a shop window admiring a period dress, beaded and cut on the bias. Pure Mansfield. Why shouldn't she buy it? After all, in London she had her KM bike. Occasionally she mounted it and rode about perched high. It was an ancient Raleigh, manufactured about the time Katherine first came to London. Maybe it wasn't just her body that was beginning to fray at the edges. She had started picking her nose too. And whenever she saw a bird she thought it was some kind of crazy omen.

She bent down to study the price tag, but it was coyly hidden from sight. Probably cost as much as six weeks in a London clinic.

You wouldn't have been able to afford it either, would you K?

My pa-man gave me a monthly allowance which he thought sufficient, which in *his* day it might have been. On one occasion he came all the way to the Riviera to take me out for a spin, joking all the time, talking Maori down the speaking tube to his chauffeur. Before he went back to New Zealand he presented me with an orchid.

Why didn't you tell him you were desperately broke? You can't eat orchids.

Pride, Norah.

He built you a concrete bus shelter somewhere in Wellington, as a memorial. I think he was trying to tell you he would have sheltered you in life, if you'd only asked.

K's laugh was not a Bloomsbury titter but the purest, uproarious colonial.

My pa-man was perfect in every way. Except he had no imagination.

I'm thinking of writing something, for radio, based on your indiscretion with the dentist. You met him in Bandol towards the end of 1915, remember? He offered you the best cure for your rheumatism. You went off for the day together, just the two of you, to a little hill village that looked like a Dürer. You went deep into the canopy of the forest ... There was such suspicious reticence about this adventure in your usually fulsome letters.

K recoiled from Norah. This was vulgar prying into her past, and she began to mock Norah's crassness, her general lack of style. Norah was just the type of colonial she had always shunned; an embarrassing relative. As for her shoes, they were so down-at-heel anyone coming up behind her on the escalator would think she was Charlie Chaplin.

Yes, she should do something about her appearance. If only she were exquisite in all things, like La Mansfield.

In the Fashion Department Norah inspected a strawberry-coloured dress with a dropped waist. She was drawn to it as to a softer self, one who had not had to struggle so hard against such biting winds, whose child was bright-eyed and doing well at some form of higher education.

She bought the dress with the last of her money and a pair of dark glasses, changing into her new gear at once. The mirror reflected a new self, sensual and slightly tanned; the sidelong glances that betrayed uneasiness concealed behind dark blue lenses. Going down the next flight a man on the adjacent escalator shot her a 'fly me' look.

She wished she'd worn them earlier in the day. Vitek would have treated her differently. A little more romantically than May I Have the Next Quick Fuck With You?

In the food hall she stared at the fruit display. How would Katherine react to it? All the fruits of the world were tumbling out of a giant cornucopia, their shine and colour showing no trace of worms or blight, but the flavour would be less delectable than in her day.

An assistant told her she'd have to buy if she kept on fingering the produce. Norah asked for a kilo of strawberries, for her brother. She couldn't put it off any longer. He would lend her the necessary. Then she wouldn't have to sell *Lyrebird*. As Norah moved towards the Exit, K faded away somewhere over in perfumery.

Rufus let the lawn mower drop. His sister was coming up the path, her face shining, while a taxi did a U-turn outside.

He was invaded by strawberry odours and when they broke the hug she gave him a quirky smile. 'I was hoping you'd ask me to dinner. I've brought the dessert.'

Installing her on the verandah, he ran off to get the welcoming drink. When he returned, she was leaning over the ledge gazing down at Pittwater, Lion Island and Palm Beach.

'God!'

'You've seen it all before, darl.'

'I never get used to it.'

'Nor do I.'

She followed the progress of a launch on its way over to the island where Tilly Devine once ran a brothel. Mother had told them about Tilly Devine, a name they would chant over and over. It had been rough and ready out here then, but now Pittwater was prime real estate: that combination of bush and water so magnetic to the Australian soul. Rufus on top of the hill had it all: bush, water, surf, beach, coves, cliffs, islands and the huge endlessly amusing sky.

A kookaburra landed on the ledge with a leafy twig in its beak, deposited it next to Norah, and stood there gazing and nodding at Rufus.

'He comes for the cocktail hour,' said Rufus who gave him a titbit.

Norah picked up the twig. 'What a wonderful omen this is!'

'He could hardly carry that and a bit of bacon, now could he? Look, what's going on? Is Sophie okay? You can't just return without warning like this, so suddenly, unless ... '

She went over to where she'd plonked her belongings on a wicker chair and extracted a book, slipping the twig reverently between its pages.

'I didn't know you went in for magic charms, Norah. That was one of Mum's books, wasn't it?'

'I'm doing some research on Mansfield. Checking facts.'

'For the BBC? She came from New Zealand.

Shouldn't you go to Wellington?'

The sky was turning to gauze. Soon the rest of the family would return. She didn't have much time to strike. She looked at him standing there, so pliant and handsome. So positive about everything. There wasn't a morbid bone in his body. Perhaps he had loathed his boarding school so much (nastier even than the one that his big sisters went to) that it rid him of any instinct for further unhappiness. He was a peace-maker. Whenever she tried to harangue him about her difficulties with Alex, he'd said how splendid their big sister was, so much less selfish than either of them. When she persisted, he'd get instant migraine, his only sign of any vulnerability.

'No, I'm not doing this for the BBC. It's a private project. I should really go to New Zealand but – well, I need money.'

Rufus smiled at her and handed her the olives.

'I'm in debt, darl, money trouble, as a matter of fact. Worse than ever. I haven't even told Bella the half of it.'

Norah turned away, blinking at the scenery. 'Everyone thinks because you're famous you must be rich.'

'I might make a comeback on the money front. I've got a brilliant new idea for a TV series. But I need a backer to make a pilot because my last series bombed. I think I've got hold of one. He's coming to dinner tonight, as a matter of fact. So be nice to him. Bat your eyelashes.'

'You're the one with the eyelashes.'

Rufus had been born with a double row. Born in a caul, in the navel of the gods. He was short of money, but it was temporary. Bad timing on her part, that's all.

Somewhere a car door slammed. Children shouted. Great breakers of colour were sweeping over the universe. The sun poised itself for its daily dive into tomorrow.

Bella hesitated at the door, very tan and wearing a white top and shorts. It was always startling, her beauty; almost oriental in its delicacy. They embraced. Norah felt like a boor with her big bones, her frontier figure.

'What a surprise!'

Her sister-in-law leaned over the ledge, pointing a brown arm to a distant cove; her wooden bangle slowly slid to her elbow. 'We took the boat over there. Look, it's turning the colour of absinthe.'

In front of them were all the hues a sunset can unleash, colliding, ascending. The still sharky inland waterways were their mirror, and the surf on the north side churned it all back into solar gold. Rufus liked to be inside every cake life wheeled in. Just when he needed to settle down, this amazing house had turned up, for instance.

83

Perhaps luck really does attach itself to those insouciant souls who believe in its power, Norah thought. With doubters, like herself, it came in dribs and drabs.

Now their two sons rushed indoors struggling over a bucket of yabbies. Shorts at half mast. Sand on sunburnt skins. The direct gaze of happiness.

'Look!' They held up the bucket. 'We caught six.'

Norah peered down gravely at their treasure and saw the heaving bucket and two sets of bare feet, toes separate and straight as descending angels. These highly socialised children were not surprised to see another adult there; the mythical aunt. They stared at her, so dark against the sky's familiar fireworks.

She wanted to scoop them up and hug them, but somehow they eluded her; these big sandy boys wouldn't come to her. Strange how a grownup like her could be insulted by a cat, or a child.

Perhaps if Sophie had been brought up near her extended family it might have helped anchor her to the real world. Her magazine-fantasies of glamour and fame would have melted away. These boys had everything: kind parents, and the unfallen world.

But when Bella went to the kitchen the worm popped out of the shining apple.

'I caught the biggest yabbie, you liar.' Bluey

clawed at Billy, who held the bucket above his head and danced around the verandah. Bluey started to cry.

Norah watched these rivals in their death dance. Her sister had shown much alacrity in the same game. But it wasn't a bucket of yabbies Alex had held mockingly over her head, it was a love letter. Norah had written it in pencil on lined exercise paper, folded it into a miniature book, embroidered its binding with green knitting wool. Alex had snatched it out of her breast pocket, dancing like Billy, with the same horrible glee; then she had read it aloud at the dinner table. 'My Dearest Vitek,' she had bawled. 'My whole being yearns for you.'

Rufus brought in chairs and coils to burn against the mosquitoes. Billy stopped his tease almost in time, but Bluey was still sobbing. Rufus dropped the chairs, grabbed the bucket and sent it and its wriggling contents flying off down into the gully. 'Shut up the two of you. And go to bed. Now!'

'They're overtired,' Bella muttered when they'd slunk off, spreading out a white damask tablecloth. It was one that Mother had kept for best. But here every day was gala day.

The burning coils on the ledge smelt of all her childhood summers: boronia that Mother collected on long headland walks; thick, chewable stars seen through a mosquito net from a verandah

85

stretcher; the sea's old divine lullaby. Mother always rented holiday cottages on the edge of long wild beaches. On one beach holiday Norah had fallen out of a gum tree and sprained her arm. Expecting no maternal consolation, she had lain crying on a verandah stretcher. Then Mother had strolled out on the verandah smoking a cigarette and, lounging on the end of her stretcher, had sung 'Goodnight Sweetheart' in a thrilling dance-hall tone, stroking her sore sprained arm. Odd how she could only express her emotions in grand gestures and comic asides; like KM's mother, come to think of it, another pinned-down butterfly.

Norah helped prepare things, setting out the cutlery, mixing the dressing. Everything in the house was highly coloured. The sugar pink curtains blowing in from all the open windows competed with the evening sky. Bella had changed into a floating magenta and yellow chiffon, designed by her best friend in the rag trade.

'We've got someone coming for dinner,' Bella said. 'Rufus thinks he's going to back the new project. He's a multi-millionaire. But they're tricky, millionaires.'

Bella sailed about the kitchen, putting on an apron, slicing cucumbers in the Magimix, washing and drying the lettuce leaves; scraping the scales off fish while Norah sat on a stool chopping parsley from right to left, then cupping it all in her hand, turning it forty-five degrees and chopping it all again as Mother had taught her. She had also taught her how to iron Dad's shirts. The men in her life had changed and so had the shirts, but not the way she ironed them. She still stuck to Mum's routine, but tried not to iron shirts in front of sterner women who would, of course, despise her.

Rufus was sweeping the verandah; fixing the candles, arranging the sound system. It was high seduction. She wondered when exactly he would move in for the kill: How much money will you invest, buster? Getting money from millionaires was famously difficult. Still, to invest in a grand new TV scheme, that was something you could claim against tax. Rufus was wily, knew how to handle people and could see at once if someone was a waste of time. He would never go on struggling, hoping for conciliation, or end up with mud on his face.

She went in to say goodnight to her nephews both grumpily reading comics in twin beds. She spent longer with Bluey, the loser. His big brother was a bully, and the friction would go on from yabbies to bigger things, until they squabbled over their parents' entrails. She would not be surprised if Bluey fled to the other side of the universe. Was it really sibling rivalry that had driven her from her native shore or had she been out to punish her mother? The umbilical tangle was too hard to unravel.

Rufus told her to have another drink, bask in the afterglow. Soon she would get a good view of the stars through his telescope, see the man in the moon. 'So tell me, now, before my backer comes (you will be nice to him, won't you, darl?), what's going on in London? How's Sophie?'

She leant back in the wicker chair, which creaked. The house cat jumped on her lap; white and Persian. Stars emerged slowly through the invisible ink above. A bat rushed out of a Moreton Bay Fig tree. Odd how hard lying became with the years. The truth would only spoil the party. How's Sophie? Well, let's see. She's being held down by nurses while she has her fits. First they have to get her off Valium, which means she will suffer from *petit mal*. Then she'll be weaned off heroin, attend daily therapy groups with the other zombies. But the minute she leaves, she'll probably go straight back into the arms of Count Dracula. No, it was better to shut up and stroke the cat, for the moment.

'I wish I could lend you some money, darl, for New Zealand. Perhaps I'll have it in a few weeks, but I'm in strife with the bank manager. He even bounced a cheque this week. The success of the TV project depends on this backer. That's why I want you and Bella to charm the arse off him. Alex will lend you some cash, or Dad, I'm sure. He adores you. But, hey, I thought the BBC paid you pretty well. Have they given you leave of absence?'

'Mansfield's rather unimaginative Dad built her a concrete bus shelter as a memorial. The symbolism of that fascinates me, because he hadn't protected her enough when she was alive. I'd like to see that memorial. And speak to an old lady in a retirement home in Wellington. She's over a hundred years old! Used to be a pal of Mansfield's in the early days. Knitted her a pale blue bedjacket as protection against the English winter. She also made one for me. I reminded her of Katherine, she said. I met her a few weeks after I first arrived in London.' She looked at Rufus excitedly. 'I've still got that bed-jacket.'

'Ooh, sounds a bit like a fetish.'

Bella came in with a jar of wattle and gum leaves. The old adorable smells. Like all hybrid Australians she lived in unjoinable halves of the world; one part of her sliced off, packed in ice. She was like a woman with a husband and a lover who needs both. Wasn't it the same for KM too?

'I'm trying to write a novel,' Bella said, twirling a gum nut with her long delicate fingers.

But anyone could see she was far too happy. Every day for Bella was full of sweet juices. No arid wastes that must be deflected in elaborate fantasies. Norah plucked at the tablecloth. Perhaps if Vitek had married her when she was pregnant, she might have the same kind of ease. 'This damask cloth reminds me of the good old days, Dad bringing home the prawns, Mum in a sunny mood.'

'How's our Dad getting on up there alone in the mountains?'

'He's not so alone. He told me he didn't know what sex was until he entered his eighties.'

Powerful headlights shone through on to the verandah full of laughing people.

'That'll be him,' said Rufus, standing up. 'Now girls, do your stuff.'

Bella was prettier than her, Norah accepted that. And younger. So this very rich man would be drawn to her. But Norah knew that, in her strawberry dress and with a face that felt light on her bones, she was more than passable. It was good to be enjoying herself in this realm of light, to forget for once the Black Room. Her rotten fruit. The bill mounting up endlessly on the other side of the world.

Vitek came into the room with champagne. 'Aha. I thought I might find you here tonight, Norah. The prodigal.'

Rufus had trouble making the connection. 'Of course. You were playmates. Way back.' He almost clapped his hands. Things were turning out so well. What serendipity. His sister even looked glamorous tonight. She wasn't embarrassing him with another bloody fuckup.

Norah fell into the old habit of admiration. Rufus had been her baby. Her very first baby. She

90

had tucked him in, told him bedtime stories, usually about escape to desert islands. But sometimes he had squirmed away from her starved embrace. Perhaps she had stifled him. Perhaps she had stifled Sophie.

Vitek kissed her cheek, making her giddy, and Rufus saw they had a thing going. He could sense it. Oh, yes. This was a sweetheart deal.

Bella relaxed visibly. She had to be on guard against other women's envy but, when a woman had a man, she could let go, because then other women were too preoccupied for envy. She smiled conspiratorially at her husband, outclassing all the smiling women on Sydney verandahs that night.

Vitek had changed into a white suit with a black cotton shirt. No tie. Little black hairs curled out between the cracks of his shirt. Bella went off to get the hommos and the cut vegetables.

'I like these old mosquito coils. Smells bring things back.' Vitek smiled aggressively at Norah, a reference to her mother's infidelity in the hut, perhaps. Or a chuck under the chin from the randy squire. She felt a spurt of resentment. But what was the point of pride; it would only spoil things. And why shouldn't I have pleasure tonight? A scene of passion on the beach. It would be an apotheosis to be with him once more at night on a North Shore beach, lying in the sand with the same hairy migrant who would murmur Thankyou, thankyou in his thrilling foreign accent. Yes, Poland was still there somewhere under the affable Aussie veneer.

The sun was seething into the horizon. How sexy sunsets were. Her eyes set into Vitek's eyes. His shudder delighted her. His extra weight was a bonus. She was far gone, always had been; much further out than he knew and not waving but drowning.

She broke the eye-lock and smiled down into her glass. She wanted this night to be the jewel she could wrap up in a piece of old silk, negotiable one day in the market of misery; that was KM's phrase for moments like this. Just for tonight Norah tried to dismiss KM from her thoughts but soon gave up the struggle and let her sit on the verandah ledge, wrapped up like the night sky in blacks and silvers, her perfume of flowering gorse filling the world.

The lights of a motorboat returning from Lion Island flashed on the verandah. Vitek slapped his neck where black hairs had started to turn white. 'Trouble with these old-fashioned coils, they don't keep away the new vicious mossies.'

'Mossies can give you Aids,' said Bella quoting the famous tabloid headline, and everyone laughed, except Norah, for she could hear KM hammering away at her.

Are you letting them get away with all this bonhomie while Sophie's locked away in a bin, withdrawing from heroin and Valium, foaming at the mouth? Are you forgetting you had to take your daughter to a clinic to see if she had Aids? The baby who was born on a bright day full of strawberries and mating pigeons, that June morning in London, she deserves a life.

No, she had not forgotten. How could she forget how Sophie had whimpered, walking round and round in tighter and tighter circles waiting for them to ring back with the results. Her daughter, her skin grey as over-pummelled dough, shivering with fear. There would be blindness, madness perhaps, incontinence. Everyone would need a special towel. No one would visit them; the house of the leper. But the results were negative.

When Sophie was a baby, Norah had borrowed a cradle from friends whose son had grown out of it. He who had been blessed with such a nice father and mother, a solid base, siblings, had also lately joined the monstrous regiment of junkies. That cradle had been cursed.

Vitek plucked a spray of wattle and reached over to twirl it in Norah's hair. He smiled wolfishly. She took in his smell, then floundered, retreating nervously. He looked away. There, she'd mucked up an important moment again; what an idiot she was. A lousy mother. A lousy lover. But then – the thought came like a benediction – she was always blaming herself; it was her bad angel speaking, always wanting to punish her and put her down.

Listen to the bright angel. To your bosom friend, Katherine Mansfield. I'm not such a bad person, I'm kind, attractive and brave. In fact, damn it, people are lucky to know me. What's the point of taking it on myself, torturing myself endlessly for what happened. It happens to kids who have a steadfast father. It happens to kids who have never been spoiled rotten. It's poison and completely democratic.

'When we've done this TV series and made a bomb, we'll do one about your Katherine Mansfield,' suggested Rufus gaily. 'Nice story. Young girl leaves colonies at sixteen. Gets caught up in the London literary set. Friend of the Lawrences. Tea with Virginia Woolf. Husband a creep. Rushes off to France in wartime. Has love affairs. Then all that Gurdjieff stuff. Very New Age. The death in Fontainebleau. Good period costumes. Bella will do the locations. Can't fail.' He filled up everyone's glass. 'Norah is writing another book about her. I'm not sure we *need* another one. Why didn't you let us know you were coming to Sydney? We would have met you at the airport. Arranged a party. Sneaking in like this. You must go and see Alex. I know she's formidable and makes you feel morally inferior, but she is your sister. At least one of us did something *really* useful with our lives.'

Now's your chance. Throw the vitriol. It was the dark angel again or was it K's wise voice?

Anger is good for you; sluices out the toxins.

'I've got some problems I have to clear up,' Norah said cautiously.

'She's being mysterious,' said Rufus. 'Let's give her a few more drinks. Let it all hang out.'

'You'll be saying Far out! next and Wow! and then I'll divorce you. I should never have married an old hippie.' Bella laughed.

'The king of the hippies,' said Vitek.

After the fish, Rufus did his pitch on the proposed TV synopsis. Then came the fruit salad and Vitek's brandy. It was the same drop he kept at the office to enjoy after sex.

Rufus said, 'I'll meet you tomorrow and show you the costing sheets.'

So that was how it was done, smooth as the change of the surf into the flat, treacherous waters of the bay. Rufus should have taken up big-game fishing. She giggled. But her revenant was still hovering, egging her on to wholesome anger, casting a blight, like any sulker at a party. It ate into the skin of her arms. Or was that a mosquito biting?

Rufus was humming now. 'Like a joint anyone? It's okay if you just take it occasionally, like brandy. So don't go into one of your tirades, Norah.'

Adrenalin started pumping through her. She was like a bitch whose litter had been killed, except for the one. Like all her female ancestors, she should have had ten or more children and spread love evenly over them all like Vegemite. But Sophie had had to take the full ferocity of her motherhood: a hot wind that stunts the sapling. Clytemnestra murdered Agamemnon in the bath because he had sacrificed her daughter to get fair winds for Troy. It must have been as easy as slicing onions; there would have been a kind of joy in it.

She could confront Rufus now, wrench him away from his deals, and lecture him. Listen, you helped promote this permissive crap, this drug culture morass they're all sinking in. Well, didn't you? You helped spread the gospel: turn on, tune in, drop out and do it in the road. Society doesn't change all by itself. It's like a rhinoceros; it needs a whole team to push it over; heave-ho, over we go. You were one of them, you bastard.

She stared at him now as he sat exhaling his marijuana, used cautiously on special occasions. The problem is he is very nice, a bit romantic, if that's a crime (it is a crime). A bit non-confrontational. But he has his excuses, his equivocations.

'Here, darl, have a puff. It won't bite.'

She started up, attacked by coughing, flinching as if from a goblet of poison. But she gulped more alcohol. 'Rufus, you know very well that it *can* bite. After its first soft nibbles, it sticks its fangs into their throats and turns them into zombies. They're vampires, but without the drive.'

She was speaking in a strange, strangled voice, slapping her arms. 'Some punch themselves with holes – even in their own eyes – and steal and lie and sell their bodies, and there are thousands and thousands of them out there.'

Anger wasn't her special gift, not outward anger anyway. Her pulse beat too violently. Her head reeled.

Rufus gave her the first look of scorn he had ever given her. 'I never encouraged kids to inject, if that's what you're wittering on about. Get your facts right, at least.'

'But, Rufus. You were a teenage idol.'

Rufus laughed. His sister was a bore, a drag, and she got it all wrong. 'I was a teenage idol. Great title for a movie.'

She hiccuped and bent closer, peering into him as into a fishbowl, watching the goldfish lights in his pissed-off eyes. 'When you started this consciousness-expanding bullshit, I begged you to reconsider; not to promote that crap from the States. But you were having your fifteen minutes of fame. You were riding the wave. No, that's wrong ...' She stood up. The stars wobbled in their sockets. KM's scarf flew off into the silver and black sky. 'You made the bloody wave, Rufus.'

When she fell on the floor and the bowl of sauce fell with her, slopping on her new silk dress,

Rufus said, 'Maybe it's jet-lag. We'd better put her to bed.'

'It's her daughter,' Vitek said, standing up wearily. 'She's a drug addict. On heroin. Nearly at death's door. She's got to pin it on someone. Otherwise she's just got herself to blame. Or her genes.' He looked speculatively at his unused violinist's hands, twisting the defunct wedding ring thoughtfully. 'Could be that kids without fathers don't prosper.' Bats flew out of the Moreton Bay Fig tree and shuddered off into the dusk.

A pigeon hopped in to the railway cafe and flew up to the ceiling, butting at the girders. Norah was ashamed of her last night's outburst. Rufus was a utopian, that's all. Utopians assume everyone will do the right thing, they don't believe in Murphy's Law.

She sipped at her coffee, glaring about her so others would avoid the madwoman's table. It had come to her in the night when she woke up on the stretcher, dry-mouthed, ashamed, that from the moment of birth Sophie had been an extension of herself. If she had given birth to a boy, she would have looked at his genitals, looked into his eyes and seen a separate creature. ('Who are you? Tell me about yourself.') And he would have looked at her assessingly, interviewing her for the top job. But right from the start, Sophie was an appendage. That was her crime. It was not all the fault of the accessibility of drugs.

The pigeon flew directly above her. It would undoubtedly shit in her coffee. It reminded her of that dark, prophetic bird, in London, a raven. Jesus, had it told her the truth. It had singled her out in Regent's Park and walked along beside her, its head drooping like a mourning relative. She couldn't shake it off, and she had known it then: bad news was on its way.

Sure enough, that evening the latest boy-friend told her the truth. There was always a new ruined boy hanging around her daughter; a new squat somewhere, invariably painted black. He imparted the news on the telephone: 'I thought you knew. She's been shooting up for ages.'

No, she hadn't known. She had been lulled by all the lies and cover-ups, telling herself sadly that Sophie was just silly, had a hole in her head.

She hung up and staring at the wall she lost her faith in life. It fell away from her like the lining of an old overcoat.

Sophie turned up that night on the scrounge, in torn fishnets, swaying on chipped stilettos, smiling falsely through the toxic shimmer.

Norah concealed her new dark knowledge and cheerfully let her in; no scolding this time; no appeals to reason; no puzzlement. Sophie was a junky. Screamingly obvious. She had been, as they say, 'in denial' all this time.

They sat on opposite armchairs, Sophie spinning lies about why she was broke, why she had lost a job again.

'It's all right, Sophie. Relax. You don't have to lie to me any more. I know you're on heroin.'

'That's a fucking lie. Who said that? I know who said it. He's a bugger. I hate him. I'm leaving him. He's the junky.'

'You both are, darling.'

'I fucking well hate you, Mother. You always think you're so right. Always so bloody right.'

She got up and strode out of the room. A few moments later the front door banged. She would be back. She needed money. Besides, in her haste to retreat, she had left her awful plastic handbag behind. Norah rifled through it and found a diary in which she read the addresses of dealers; the amounts Sophie had scored and sold. She closed her eyes. Sophie might as well have been brought up in an orphanage, in the gutter, in a ghetto. She could not have turned out worse. All the years of taking her to the dentist, nursing her through measles and mumps, putting off dates because there was no suitable babysitter, paying for piano lessons, taking her on holidays, what had that been for?

The doorbell would ring again soon. Sophie would come back for her incriminating handbag. And tomorrow she would get her to the doctor, by brute force if necessary. Then she recalled the few moments that had elapsed between Sophie stalking out of the flat and banging the front door: just enough time for her to steal from her mother's purse.

The purse, of course, was not under the hall mirror where she always left it. And her twenty pounds had gone missing; more than enough to score a bit of heroin at the pub.

She slumped against the wall, staring dully around at the furniture, the flowers, the view of the garden, all so tasteful, acquired through years of hard graft. What had Sophie gained from all this civilisation, that rat scuttling through back alleys looking for more shit? Sweet fuckall.

She knew at last what she had to do. She went out into the garden and found a long stick blown off the ash tree in the last November gales.

A woman upstairs popped her head out the window. 'Nice and mild for this time of the year, isn't it?'

Norah smiled up at her. The smile tore her face.

She slashed the stick through the nice mild air. She had always tried to teach by kindness, by example. But she had been stupid. Learning involved pain.

She came back indoors, locked the French windows, sat down and waited, her stick lying on the table. She stared at the stick. At boarding school in the mountains she had waited and waited, waited forever as she was waiting now; just one of the guard of honour lining the drive for the ceremonial visit of the Admiral of the Fleet. But he was very late. A scalding trickle of piss ran down her legs then like the burning tears running down her cheeks now as she waited for her daughter.

The bell rang. Sophie stood there with her stoat's eyes, a ghastly simper failing to hide her fear. 'I left my handbag, Mummy.'

Smiling with deceitful vagueness, Norah followed her into the room where the bag was perched and picked up the stick. She raised it over her head and began to thrash her baby, she who had never been slapped in her life.

'You stole my money.' Down came the stick. A stunned Sophie began to scuttle around like a snake. 'To buy drugs.' Whack. The snake crawled under the big table. 'You're a junky.' Whack. 'And a liar.' Whack. 'And probably a prostitute.'

'I'm not a prostitute, you mad fucking bitch ...'

Norah crouched down, hitting away at her under the table. Sophie pleaded for mercy, hunched herself up into the foetal position and moaned, but Norah showed no mercy. Sophie got away and dashed out towards the French windows, rattling the handles and kicking the glass, dodging and weaving back across the room while the cane whistled down on her, landing mostly on her shoulder-pads. All the time Norah had a rictus grin on her face; she was killing the snake of her disappointment. But it slithered away through the other door, hissing back at her: 'You stupid old cow. You can't even hit straight. I didn't feel a thing.'

A woman in Bradford kept a chain permanently around her waist with a twenty-five yard extension which was padlocked to her son, an addict and a punk. He could roam the council flat, he could go to the lavatory, he could sit in the other room and watch TV, but he couldn't go out and score. She admired that woman.

The next day, on their way to the doctor's (the first of so many doctors, so many false dawns), Sophie lay curled up in the corner of the taxi, a grey foetus, and said, 'I bet you wish you'd had an abortion.'

Norah held her child's cold hands and stared at them. Then came the usual maternal flow of comforts. Her life had been just a jerky old black and white movie until Sophie was born; she didn't know how deep she was until she had a baby. And so on and on. The foetus didn't react.

Now here she was, back home, on the other side of the world, worn out with trying and yet still trying.

She fixed the silly pigeon with a superstitious stare. Everything depended on whether it had enough sense to fly out of the wide open door and back into the dirty freedom.

EIGHT

'Never go to the public bar on your own. They're a rough mob,' Dad had barked often enough.

She put down her bag with a thump on the beer-soaked pavement. Today the troops were bloody well going to disobey. The train journey had been slow and boring with blackened scrubland on either side of the tracks still steaming from the bushfires. Her head throbbed. She had achieved nothing in Sydney except to make a buffoon of herself.

Self-contempt was destructive, the worst emotion. She would never have thought herself intrinsically evil: would never have imagined that anything bad could come from inside her. Sophie, her fruit, had smelt like a peach orchard when she was born.

Seen from the blazing footpath the smoky pub had an inviting quality. Both doors were wedged open to catch the big spenders from the village fete now noisily in progress. She entered the forbidden zone, peering towards the spot where Dad had his reserved stool. Mercifully he was absent.

It was an unreconstructed Aussie bar room for the boys, even though the law allowed the ladies, and a few tousled female boozers did hang about, largely ignored until closing time. A drunken lumberjack was hugging the battered jukebox which pelted out a Janis Joplin song, the one about windscreen wipers slapping time to her and Bobby McGee. Notices of imminent Prawn Nights, coach trips to Sydney and the sale of unwanted items including livestock were displayed on the wall along with the inevitable pin-ups.

She ordered a genteel middy among the brawny schooner drinkers and in the tiny deadly silence that ensued decided to slink into a corner and take refuge in KM. Anything rather than face the great gloomy house with Dad in it.

The sound of the wind is very loud in this house. The curtains fly. There are strange pointed shadows, full of meaning, and a glittering light upon the mirrors. Now it is dark – and one feels so pale – even one's hands feel pale, and now a wandering broken light is over everything. It is so exciting, so tiring, too; one is waiting for something to happen.

'Come up for the fete?' roared a voice.

106

Looking up she saw two blokes. Her interrogator was wearing a shirt emblazoned with the words: NUTS, SCREWS, WASHES AND BOLTS.

She smiled vaguely. 'My Dad lives here, up the hill.'

'We can walk up the hill, can't we, Jeff?'

The darker man whose face was brick coloured gave her the once-over. Maybe she was dying for it. Bit of an old boiler, but still tasty. His T-shirt had the more sober message: CENTACOM.

'I'm laying cables up the hill. Want me to lay you a cable?'

They both spluttered over that one. He looked healthy; well grazed, no sign of foot-and-mouth, probably no hydatids. As for her, basically she supposed she must seem very stud and matronly, like the ewe advertised for sale up there on the wall. Why not take him up the hill? Shoo Dad out of the way and make the old timbers shudder. Drive away the bogies of grief and self-loathing. But it wouldn't work. It would be just nuts, screws, washes and bolts.

She got up and moved towards the bar to order another middy when through the door trotted a tall brown mare decked like its rider in red and blue rosettes. The crowd handed up a schooner to the winner of the gymkhana, and tried to pour beer down the horse's throat as it twitched its flanks, flared its nostrils, and rolled its eyes madly in their sockets until it finally spluttered beer all over its persecutors. To ride a horse into a crowded pub was a genial act of cruelty. But she couldn't rescue the horse as she had once rescued the worm; well, not exactly rescued it, but put it out of its misery. One afternoon at boarding school she had seen a crowd of girls around one of the wooden benches. They had let her come closer so she could join in their medical experiment. They had been skinning a worm alive. Her foot had lifted itself up without any orders from her brain and squashed the worm flat. She'd had to pay for that, of course.

Over in a corner of the bar she saw a slouching, familiar figure, an empty seat beside him.

'You came up to see the Raj station, Pete.'

'I like to keep moving.'

'Didn't the boss treat you right?'

'Standing there, stacking the dishwasher all day. That's no life. The sea flashing outside just tantalises yer.'

'So what are you up to?'

'I've still got that broken heart.'

She glanced down at his crotch before she could prevent herself and nodded condolences for the absent sperm and the absent wife who'd run off after his vasectomy. 'You'll meet a nice fresh mountain girl.'

'These mountain girls want kids. They won't

adopt. Silly, isn't it? All those orphans hanging around in institutions.'

On the floor beside him was a battered brown suitcase. He kicked it. 'All me worldly goods is in there. Nowhere to store it, but it slows a feller down when he's looking for work. Doesn't look good. Looks as if you might be moving on too quick.'

'You can store it in our garage.'

'Done! Let's drink on it.' He edged his way cockroach-like through the beefier types who were now drifting back to the bar and instantly got Mr Flood's attention.

She was the only woman amid all this seething testosterone: the Ab who had only one sock on; the drunk who jogged his hangovers away every morning, risking death on the Great Western Highway; the cattle farmer from the valley whom she'd met at one of her mother's Christmas parties.

'Hello, Norah. I didn't think your Dad let you come near this place.'

'Isn't he sweet?' Somebody shoved her and her book dropped to the filthy floor.

The farmer picked it up. 'Careful you don't spill beer on it. It's a first edition, isn't it?'

When he gave the book back, she smiled at him radiantly.

'You should come and visit us, Norah. Come mushrooming – er, the two of you.' He looked at

Pete with puzzled interest. 'The weather has never been better for it. We'll go around on the tractor. There's loads of flannel flowers this year. Your Mum used to love them.'

'Whenever I go to watch the sunset from Pulpit Rock I can see right down into your farm. The bush looks much lusher than I can ever remember it.'

'It was all those fires. We've got the new growth from the singed bark. A few flowers need fire to germinate ...'

He had a sandy, stockman's face, but recently he'd fallen off his bike. There'd been that and now the low cattle prices and then vandals shot the udders off one of his best milkers. But he could still stand there, waving his freckled hands, instructing her in the mysteries of waratahs.

'Fire flowers,' she murmured happily. Why hadn't she been loved by a man like that?

All the way to the top of the hill Pete lagged behind, one finger pressed over the faulty catch of his suitcase. Flushed children holding kewpie dolls from the fete were crying in the crowded backs of cars, their cheeks sticky with fairy floss. Pop band pulsations, the thwack of the wood-chopping and wild gusts of cheering flew around their heads.

At the wrought-iron gates she paused while he handed over his precious case.

'Pick it up before next week when I'll be off to London. Good luck finding a job, Pete.'

But he hung around, kicking the gravel. 'You've got funnel web spiders here. You oughta pour kero down the holes, or is it meths?'

'See you later.'

'Aren't we going mushrooming in the valley? That bloke said we could go down tomorrow. I've never been mushrooming in me life.'

She sighed. 'I'll borrow Dad's car. Meet you at the pub, then, at about two.' She turned away and carried the wretched case up to the house and the seven creaking steps on to the Dad-filled verandah.

Dad put down his newspaper, foiled of his T-bone steak every fete day because of the overcrowding. 'What's that rubbish? I heard you plotting something. You haven't been picking people up at the fete?'

'A friend's suitcase. He used to do odd jobs for Mum when we lived in Curl Curl. Peter Duck. I said we'd store it for a few days while he looked for work.'

'No.'

'But, Dad. He can't be lugging this old thing about. It's bad for his image.'

'No.'

'Well at least let me have a cup of tea. Have you seen Laurel lately?'

'Better take that case back to Mr Duck, dear, before he disappears. He should pay storage fees at a warehouse. Bludging on me.'

'But, Dad, it's only *space*.'

It was hopeless. Dad believed everything in the world was somebody or other's property. He didn't even like strangers *looking* at the house. He thought they wore it out by looking, by scouring away at it with their eyes.

She threw down her purse and bag and picked up the suitcase. By the time she got to the gate, however, Pete was an ant at the bottom of the hill. Someone had lost a silver helium balloon and it was floating fast up towards her. Oh, bugger Dad. She lurched into the garage where his old Holden was parked and hid the case right at the back behind the tins of oil and diesel. She didn't hate her father; not at all. She just had to be sly. Tyrannies impose it.

The gates of *Lyrebird* were unlocked at last. Open wide. She walked right in up the curving path. Heat shimmered on wilting grass. A magpie dipped out of the pine. Her niece was in the garden hanging up the clothes. She looked up, pegs in her

112

mouth. Beyond was the little shed and the white rock overlooking the valley. When could she claim them? Never now.

Justine finished pegging up the pillowslip. 'I've been expecting you, Auntie Norah.'

'Have you been at the fete?'

'I was one of the witches in the broom-throwing contest. I saw you walk up from the railway. The others are still there.'

Her niece must have rushed home to tidy up. Guilty about last time.

'Where did you disappear to, Justine?'

'I thought my marriage was over.' A sudden wind flapped a sheet into her face. Her features loomed through it like a ghost's. 'Oh, shit, now it's covered in make-up. I wanted to warn you not to buy anything from the home-made wines stall. Bloke down the road did and it exploded all over his kitchen.'

Norah stared over her head to the top of the shed which she could just glimpse at the edge of the garden. It was battered but just the right size for a study. That would be the place to work on the KM idea.

'I'll just finish hanging this lot up.'

Norah left her and strolled towards the shed, stood there for a moment looking down on to the valley and the long plateau with its crooked lines of apple trees. All the love that

113

she had harboured for her mother and father between the ages of six and ten had discharged itself over that orchard and dripped deep into the folds of the Kanimbla valley. She knelt down and touched the white rock. A jolt of regret passed through her. She had always imagined she would spend years hanging about this house. Wishful thinking, no doubt.

The shed was full of rusting gardening stuff, but she could clear all that, mend the rotting fly screens, move in a small wooden table and chair, and there she would sit for infinity, facing outwards, drinking in the labyrinthian blues then close her eyes, and the dead would dictate it all: KM's fatal day on the beach, the lonely soldier, the knock on her door, the dentist, their passion. She could smell the secret rising from the letters, as strong as a burnt saucepan. Strange that Middleton Murry never picked it up. The dentist kept postponing his return to London because he wanted to remain with her (a mere acquaintance!) over Christmas. But the clincher was in the confession to her friend (Koteliansky). She told him she was mad with joy. She had given her heart 'freely, freely'.

'Hey, dreamer. What about some tucker?'

It was Justine, standing in the magnolia shadows, watching her with a little smile.

They went back and sat in the shadowy

kitchen, its shutters wide open to the shining day.

'You look well, Justine. A bit like Granny, you know.'

Her niece had the big bones of the family, but her eyes were too faraway and romantic. When she had finally married an engineer, it was recognised as an extremely sensible move. Perhaps too sensible. Maybe she had been too young to clip those burning wings.

'The marriage is on again. He's so easy and nice all the time he drives me to it.'

'To what?'

'Bad behaviour. I'm bad for both of us. I married a nice guy, you see, that's my problem. He's down at the fete now minding the baby. Mum's there too, by the way, helping on the Red Cross stall.' Justine gave Norah an assessing look. This tension between her mother and her aunt was a pain in the arse.

'Ah, yes. Alex.'

'Mum's a bit hurt that you haven't contacted her.'

'I'll see Alex soon. But this is just a rushed business trip.'

'Oh. A business trip. But you saw Rufus didn't you? And Dad?'

While Justine's back was turned, while she was getting something out of the oven, Norah stuck the knife in. 'I'm desperately short of money. I've got to sell this house, I'm afraid, or I'll be in debtor's prison.'

Justine did not look up from the oven. 'Perhaps we could buy it?'

Norah felt something like jealousy. If she could not have *Lyrebird*, nobody should have it. Nobody that counted.

'Well, I'm going to want the maximum for it. I'm going to put it in professional hands.'

Justine swung around, dropping the oven-cloth, her eyes flinty. 'Of course you will. No special favours for members of the family. Right?'

The next day Norah drove down the hill to meet Pete. She parked the Holden by the pie shop, then crossed the highway and looked into the pub. Mr Flood, the proprietor, stopped polishing glasses. 'Just looking for someone,' she said.

Dad emerged from the toilet aghast. In ceremonial silence he opened the outside door and followed her out on to the pavement. 'Anything wrong? Has Laurel phoned me?'

'I was just looking for someone.'

'You're not picking people up in the pub,' he said, banging his stick.

'No, no, nothing like that. Go back and finish your T-bone.'

'Airy-fairy,' he called out obscurely as she went back across the highway. Or was it so obscure? Dad was smarter than she thought. What he meant by airy-fairyness was the fey, almost dislocated behaviour of people under too much pressure: the madwoman of the mountains who walked about with unbrushed hair and odd socks, who masturbated on the idea of being *en rapport* with a dead genius. Pathetic.

To hell with Pete. He was like that hanky she picked up under a restaurant table in Manly then threw away because it was so squalid.

He emerged from the pie shop, a brown paper bag in his hands. 'So we wouldn't starve,' he said, settling in beside her.

'Any luck finding work?'

'Something's in the wind. It's fixing up those old handrails and footpaths under the waterfalls. Not much money. Man in the pub put me on to it.'

'It's dangerous work.' A horrible smell permeated the car. 'Throw away those meat pies. They kill their own meat.'

Shouts of the farmer's children echoed beyond the ridge. One of the dogs had followed them, letting his master go back and start the barbecue, barking intermittently at Pete.

117

'He senses my innate evil.'

She giggled. A bit of menace would have improved him. Shorts that revealed knobbly knees. A shirt too big for him. He was unprepossessing as he stooped and plucked, the third man in the gangster movie, the dumb stooge.

'Reckon we can take as much as we can carry.'

They had already filled one box and were half way into another. The smell was voluptuous, the touch carnal. Every now and then she stopped and stretched, brushing off blowflies, gazing at the sloping land, the Sanskrit on the scribble-gums, the curious luminosity of mushrooms before they're picked. This lot had sprung up overnight although there were hardly any cattle droppings. The herd seldom strayed so far from the farm. This was not the Australia she had known as a child. But she had known it was here.

She looked up high above her to the cutting edges of the ramparts. Boarding school had been on that plateau somewhere. Funny to think she had once stood up there, transfixed, staring longingly down here, feeling the strange tingle of absolute beauty. One day she had blown up a red balloon and tied a message to it: one single word, 'Help!' She had sent it flying off like a pigeon down towards this same magical valley from which rescue must surely come. And although it had floated

118

down in the right direction it had soon got caught in a banksia bush and burst, hanging there for weeks, a red shred, bitten at by birds.

'Want a fag?'

She shook her head. But sat down with him while he had a smoke.

'You look a bit down in the dumps,' he said after doubling up under a chain-smoker's cough.

'Oh. I thought I was a cheerful soul.'

'Nah, something biting yah. You got something on yer mind.'

Tears were not her metier. Somehow, they had never been an option. Perhaps it was the strict upbringing. Now like a torpedoed submarine, water swamped the control deck. Tears gushed from each eye.

'Well, you recently had a bereavement in the family,' he said gently.

'That was nearly three years ago. It's not that ... my daughter's a drug addict.'

When he reached for another cigarette, his hands were trembling. He was an old softie; his eyes had not lied about that. 'You must have been through hell and back.'

Then she was off again. Howling. Yes. To hell and back, like Demeter. The blue cattle dog put his head on her feet. She was speaking his language. Even the flies laid off. When she spoke again, she was panting; the words came in a fierce

119

torrent, each phrase shooting out like a dagger bouncing back from her tormented mother's heart.

'It's not just the waste and horror, it's all the squalor: the forged cheques, police summonses, endless deceits. Oh, it goes on and on. Everything I try goes wrong. Her godmother lent her a piano because she had been so promising. I thought it might do the trick. But one of her hangers-on took an axe to it. *An axe!*' Norah let out a crazy laugh. 'When she was chucked out of that flat, I went back to fetch the piano and there it was, splattered with bright blue paint and with a huge gash in its side. When I touched the keys, there was no sound. Nothing. The piano had been disembowelled. All that wiring, all those little hammers, *everything* had been taken out. They had sold it to a scrap metal merchant to buy drugs. I had to go down to the docks and argue with the guy for hours to get it back. It cost a fortune.'

In Pete's mind the piano was Norah's daughter, splattered with blue paint, a huge axe wound in her side, her insides all taken out; all her notes mute.

He gazed regretfully at the mushrooms, which were fast losing their lustre.

'She sold everything: my lamp, my sheets, my earrings, her special birthday watch from Grandma. One day I saw her staggering in the street wearing torn fish-net tights and giving off a sort of awful phosphorescence, a ghastly shine like rotting fruit. When I went up to her, there was this stench coming from her, and she didn't know who I was. She wasn't there.' Norah rocked back and forth, once more Demeter grieving for Persephone.

'In Soho I saw a young woman, obviously an addict, crash on the footpath. Everyone else walked by. I phoned the ambulance from a public box, but they sent the cops. When they came in their paddy wagon, they handled her with such contempt, I kept thinking, It's worse than rape.

'Maybe you run out of respect for the human race. In their job.

'Then, at last, fear of Aids, or maybe she'd had enough, she *asked* for help. I went to the latest squat, but her boyfriend barred my way. 'Who's this old tart?' he said. My daughter said, 'You're talking about my mother.' I stared at him for a long time and then I understood. He wanted me to rescue him as well; he wanted to suck my dugs. There was no one for him, you see, no resources at all. He was a street boy. I could feel him begging me. And I just – it was awful – I pushed him away, straight off the life-raft. There wasn't enough room in my heart.'

'Or in your purse.'

Norah, the emotional bag-lady, had put down her bags. 'She'd detoxed before. Time and time again. That's easy. I'm an expert. It takes five days. Then five weeks of sleepless nights. But she always slid back the minute she hit the high street.'

'Well, she's still alive!'

'I used to lie awake imagining she had been left for dead, her rotting corpse seeping through the floorboards, covered in maggots ... the telephone call at dawn from the police. Two weeks ago I finally got her into the best clinic in the country. She *wanted* to go in. Pure fear won out in the end. Maybe this time it will work. Have you seen a flowering shrub after the builders have left scaffolding on it for weeks on end? The leaves are yellow and all dead and flat but, sometimes, after a few showers of rain, it sprouts again.'

Norah stopped suddenly. There it was again. Hope, still raising its stubborn worn-out head.

Pete was used to hard-luck stories. 'It must be puzzling to have a kid like that. Especially when you always looked after it proper. One day she'll grow out of it. Not like street kids. When they go off the rails, there's no rich Mum to bail them out.'

'I've spent all my money on her already.'

'I s'pose yer old man wouldn't give you a handout. I heard the old bastard argue about the suitcase. No, he won't give you nothin'.'

'Dad believes in self-reliance. No one ever helped him.'

'Oh, listen, I wanna tell yer something. If

122

anything happens to me, if I get run over or something, you can keep them family jewels. You've been that good to me.'

She stared at him. The valley was enfolding them in pewter-greens and silver-greys. The light undulated. His eyes had such kindness in them, soft as the petals of the endangered flannel flower.

'Me heirlooms. In the suitcase. I bequeath them all to you.'

She stood up, dazed. The flies returned to the attack. 'I'm sorry to spill it all out on you.'

He helped her to her feet. If her kid ever kicked the habit, she'd be a new person, he knew that. It'd be like taking off a tourniquet after a snake bite. The blood would come rushing back to the limb and away she'd dance.

'We'll have to carry this lot back now. Beauty! A free box of mushies for nothing.'

He flicked away his stub with Humphrey Bogart panache.

She scurried after it and stamped to make sure there was no spark left.

'I'm sure you'll get that council job, Pete. They need blokes like you now. The tourist business is booming. Everyone wants to hit the old trail, camp in the blue gum forest.'

But somehow she doubted if he was up to clearing trails. He'd be better off working the greyhound tracks. Poor bugger. Would she ever shake him off now she'd dropped her load on him? Not that it mattered. She was leaving soon.

The farmer had built the house himself. He had stood about building sites watching how they did it. And then he had done it. In the middle of nowhere. Cut trees, sawed logs, poured concrete and dragged a suitable block of stone from off his land for the fireplace. The only expert he'd called in was an electrician. Now it resonated with books, pictures, family life; and the silver gums curved and danced like nymphs all around. Before eating they all had a go on the flying-fox, crashing into the creek half way across. The blue cattle dog jumped in after them.

They drove home at dusk. A kingfisher flashed low across the creek; two kangaroos, their eyes as soft as Pete's, trembled out of the bush, and she got that tingly feeling. Sometimes the world was achingly beautiful, and you just had to accept that it never led to anything. In a year or so the roos would have moved further west. The bulldozers would follow, and then the felled trees.

Dusk came in a rush. She switched on the fog-lights and sealed the window. They crawled up the steep highway; the mist seeping into the car increased the mystery of the hour, getting into their hair, covering the rear-vision mirror, leaving her tunnelling in the dark.

Pete remained silent, grimly watching the left side of the road which dropped a thousand feet to the gully. His ancestors had laid this road. She felt shy with him now. All that blubbering. But it had made her feel easier inside. She could see other things more clearly. Her succession of boy-friends over the years couldn't have made Sophie's life any easier: the French antique dealer, grinning falsely, who had bribed her with outsize dolls; the jealous English journalist who had wanted to squash her underfoot, snail-like; the student from Liverpool who had loved Sophie as much, if not more, than he had loved her (it was he who first organised those piano lessons), and the child had loved him back, eyes brimming with trust. But the student still had spots! Ah yes, she might have been a sturdy mother, but she had failed to provide an impervious nest.

She dropped Pete off at the pub without asking him about his sleeping arrangements. Mr Flood probably let him stay out the back. Or there was always that fete stall in the park. She fought off her sense of obligation. He'd survived before, that man. He'd manage now.

She went to bed early while Dad was still watching television – when she was old she would never sit alone in front of a TV set, displaying her loneliness – and snuggled under the blankets with her dear friend. She could almost recite KM's confession of love to Koteliansky:

Oh my God, I am very happy. When I shut my eyes, I cannot help smiling. You know what joy it is to give your heart freely – freely.

Such adventurousness when she was alone and consumptive. For KM, letters were oxygen. Even a complete stranger singing on a crowded street could touch her so deeply, she had to record it at once:

It clutched my heart. It flies in the wind today. One of the voices, you know, crying above the talk and the laughter and the dust.

NINE

Dad rustled the local paper irritably. Last night he'd woken up twice thinking he'd heard a prowler in the garden. There was an escaped prisoner on the loose again. He'd taken the Samurai sword down from the wall and gone out on to the lawn in his bare feet, swinging his shining blade, decapitating the shadows.

This morning there were no eggs in the chicken coop. Even though it was always padlocked at night, someone had stolen them and was probably hiding in one of the caves below, sucking away at *his* property.

Certainly there was a plunge in the level of the chicken wire. And the school signboard was in a different spot. It had probably been used as a battering ram.

The old killer was out of sorts. Frustrated. Tonight he would sleep with his sword by his side.

'When's Laurel coming up to see you, Dad?'

'She's not.'

'Oh, dear.'

'Tomorrow morning early I'm off to Sydney to see her for a day or two.'

'I've got to be off myself soon, to London.'

'You should stay here. We'll find you a man in Australia.'

She had a man in Australia. That's why she'd gone to London in the first place. But Dad was too old to be bothered with all that now. And she didn't want to set him off again about Mother and Vitek. Dad was as obtuse as Middleton Murry when it came to his wife's dalliance. But she couldn't talk. She'd been just as blind. Mother must have given Vitek a taste for older women. They were so grateful, so enthusiastic, and there was no palaver.

'Now. Don't forget to leave Andy his tea and biscuits and the five dollars I'll put on the mantelpiece, and write messages down clearly. The Returned Soldiers League might ring about the next meeting. I'm the only surviving officer in the group who served in Wewak. I've had to cancel lunch at the Gallipoli Club tomorrow because Laurel prefers the Rose Bay Golf Club. I want you to drive me to the station at eight sharp. Make sure you've cleaned the car windows. If you see the escaped prisoner, ring the police. Ring them if there's no eggs tomorrow. And don't light fires behind my back.' His voice broke over her head like the Pacific. She was still riding on his shoulders in a choppy surf out towards the billowing net.

'It says here that house prices are rising. There's a boom on. You're quite right to put your house on the market. Too big for you. I tried to stop your mother buying it. A white elephant. Invest in television shares. And buy a modern bungalow, if you must. I don't know why your mother went around buying up all these rotting Victorian houses, standing in the rain at auctions, spending the last of her father's money. We ought to sell the lot and buy a nice modern unit in Sydney.'

Dad couldn't bear to take a gamble. He liked to sit on his money. Keep it in a box. His own father had been a gambler on such an astronomical scale, and he and his brothers had suffered for it. His meanness was the usual swing of the pendulum, as was her own vagueness and insolvency.

She went outside. The red and green parrots were shrieking and pouncing. There were already early windfalls in the grass.

'You just missed your sister,' said Mrs Flood. The Flood family ran everything, even the garage and souvenir shop. Her mean eyes belied the myth that to live among nature flooded the soul with glory but,

129

with dour Mr Flood to contend with, how else could you protest but break out in shingles.

'Dad thinks the escaped prisoner might have stolen our eggs last night.'

'He'll be miles away now if he's got any sense.' Mrs Flood's smile was cynical, as if she knew the previous convictions of all her customers.

Norah hurried out with the groceries and set off for her night alone. Her leave from the BBC would soon be over and no work to show for it. A day or two of solitude and quiet might lead to some more ideas about the KM documentary, how to start it, for instance. All she had to do was to sign the form at the real-estate agents, and mission accomplished. Katherine didn't have the art of borrowing money, either.

Outside the window of the car she saw a stout young village woman (who baked the best scones at the fete) with her freckle-faced son. They were struggling along in the face of harsh, oncoming winds with an air of such innocent toughness; she never saw anything like it in London. The pre-adolescent boy with the flying ginger hair dragging his Mum behind him were the Australian archetype, mother and son, human gum trees that had never been transplanted.

Compared with them she was neurotic, her identification with KM text-book displacement, a sign of encroaching dottiness. Like her recent regression to medieval superstitions and belief in omens.

Strange that Alex hadn't dropped in or rung. She was probably waiting to see who'd make the first move; to maintain the old power ascendancy. Or perhaps she was just too busy being a saint at the local hospital.

To quell her hostility, Norah only had to remember her sister's bossy need of her. When she was about ten, she rebelled, refused to obey Alex any more. The mutiny had occurred on the corner of Manly Corso and the tension that ensued was her lifelong punishment.

Not long ago, on one of her Christmas visits, believing herself free of the old umbilical coils, she had said firmly to Alex, 'You should go and see a hypnotherapist about why you need to be so controlling. Could be you're scared stiff of something?' Her sister had stopped giving orders then, for a stunned second or two. It was as loud a silence as the sudden stopping of a hailstorm. Then the voice rattled on.

If she stayed in Australia, she would not have been able to resist her sister's will, her superior energy, and would have ended up like all those other little sisters, creeping about behind the more dynamic one.

Norah drove past *Lyrebird* where Alex was still in residence and parked the car in the garage, checking to see that Pete's case was still safely hidden behind the cans. She walked up the drive, inhaling the deep benevolence of the pines. But an electric storm was on its way. Pine cones were starting to thud on the ground. She was overcome by a wave of sexual desire. Last night she'd had a sexy dream, the first for ages, spreadeagled on the sandy shore, no Vitek in sight, just the lewd, penetrating sea.

She let herself in the back way, through the porch door with one swift, cat-deflecting movement and took refuge in the little TV room, once Mother's study, where for years and years she had written those plaintive aerogrammes full of botanical jottings. Norah had only ever given them a cursory glance. By that time romance was less compelling for Mother than planting shrubs and flowers and seeing them grow around her. This big main house without a name had been left, not to Dad, because he would have sold it and lived in lodgings, but to Alex. She was the eldest and she had stayed in Australia, except for a stint in New Guinea much later, with the mobile eye hospital. Above all she would look after Dad in his old age. All that flashy Norah had done was send back photographs of herself in exotic places.

From her deathbed Mother had written prophetically to Norah: 'You'll need the house next door one day. I feel it in my bones. But try not to sell it, darling.'

Norah ran her fingers over Mother's old

Remington typewriter. Insects nosedived into the fly screens. Perhaps it wasn't KM she wanted to bring back from the dead after all. Perhaps that was why she carried Mum's copy of K's journals around all the time.

She walked into the kitchen to make tea. Mother's tirades. Alex had them, fortissimo. Norah had them too, but usually internally, silently. She stared through the fly screens at the churning night. A cup of tea would lay the ghosts.

She went outside to empty the tea leaves on the roses. The garden tap was dripping and a shadowy figure was drinking out of cupped hands. A chill rippled down her spine. Animal fear in her own backyard.

But the shadow said, 'Hello. It's only me.' He moved closer, and she could see the familiar weasel face, his uncertain smile. 'I'm taking a liberty, I know, but this house is the nearest.'

'Nearest?'

'To the caves.'

'You've been sleeping in caves?'

'They're all right. Some camper left a few hessian bags.'

'The bushrangers used to sleep there.'

'I've been sneaking up at night, sucking them eggs, I'm afraid. Things got tight, money-wise. But I landed the job. A trial run anyhow, to see if I can take the pace. I'm gonna walk right down into the Grose Valley, and keep me eyes peeled and tell 'em what needs fixing.'

'Come on inside. Have a drink or something.'

'What about yer Dad?'

'He's away. But he'll be back tomorrow,' she said quickly, not wanting him to get too relaxed. Giving but not giving too much.

She made more tea because that was what he wanted. She started the fire, loving the sacrilege of lighting it. Where was the shortage of wood, for God's sake? They were surrounded by broken logs, fallen branches, pine cones in the grass, manna from heaven, their little feathery seeds blowing out of the cracks in the high wind; what optimism, to think they might aspire to pines.

'Dad hates me lighting fires. It's a funny quirk.'

'Scared of starting a bushfire. Don't you have a fire screen?'

'It's not that simple. He just doesn't like the prodigality of the flames. I think it must remind him of spending money. He went through the Depression. Had to go to his first job wearing his Dad's old army boots. Ate nasturtiums.'

'I'll be getting a decent wage for the council job. I'll find a room. Get me family heirlooms out of the garage. Buy a suit.'

'Look for a new wife.'

He went silent, staring into the fire. His scrunched up face opening against the heat. 'I've given that all up. It's not worth the trouble. Don't you reckon?'

She blushed. It wouldn't give her up. 'Don't give up hope,' she said heartily. 'All women don't want babies.'

'Most do,' he mourned.

She retreated into the kitchen. Women had wombs and might as well use them at least once, she supposed, or it would be dying without having done the obvious; just as well they didn't know what they were letting themselves in for.

She emerged, holding a plate of chops. 'Stay and eat something, Pete. I'll grill these.' She made lots of mashed potatoes and cooked the remaining carrots. An egg-stealer needed bulk.

Flames that rubbed their yellows together, sending out an occasional spark on to the rug which he at once stamped on, cheered him up, made him talkative. And the smell of the chops cooking.

'I was born in Bourke. Mum was a cleaner in the bar. Her Mum had been a maid. Worked in flash houses in New Zealand. I've still got a photer of her somewhere serving tea in some bloody mansion in a frilly cap. All I know about me Dad is that he was a drover. Just passing through. Big built feller. Like me if I'd eaten my spinach.'

If his grandmother had worked in a mansion

near Wellington she might have met KM!

'Did you have rickets?'

'Rickets, croup, whooping cough, you name it. Mum married again. But the new bloke didn't like me. Only to be expected. So they put me in a children's home. Then he broke his back doing army training. Spent the rest of his life in a wheelchair. Mum had to put me in a Home for two years. She was always guilty about that. But she let me move into her place in the end. I set it up nice for Pearl. When she dumped me, well, have you ever tried to get money back on stoves and saucepans?'

Looking into the flames she made out a picture of K, the adolescent genius with the fuzzy almost Maori-like hair running up the steps of a fine colonial house. The hostess kisses her, but the soulful eyes of La Mansfield reveal that she has read too much into the kiss. Her hostess is a younger version of that benefactor who had tried so hard long ago to give her K's translucent letters. The two Edwardian women stand, arms around each other's waists, looking out through the long windows. In comes Pete's Gran in her maid's uniform and cap, staggering under the weight of a silver tray. She places bread and butter on top of the top shelf of the what-not, then fills the expanding layers with dear little plates of scones, meringues, sponges and fruit cake. They sit on the Chesterfield. The hostess offers her a scone and K pours milk in her tea. Her hands are trembling.

Norah looked up at Pete sleepily. There was no way she could throw him out, especially on a night like this. A stray dog. To sleep in a cave. Anyway she owed him.

'You'd better sleep in the spare room. I'll put a bottle in for you.' He might have been Sophie the way she fussed over him.

Lying in the big house, creaking with shadows, hearing the possums scuttle on the roof, it was reassuring to think that Pete was down the corridor, even though he seemed too frail to tackle an intruder.

In the middle of the long night she thought she heard him calling out, not in anguish or in shock, but from the bowels of some impenetrable desolation. She sat up in bed, listening, but could only hear the steady drum of rain on the corrugated-iron roof. That woman had dumped Pete after his vasectomy ...

He left early after breakfast with a firm tread, looking quite presentable. She made a point of frying him up lots of illicit eggs, shoring him up for the day's hike down to the Blue Gum.

She cleaned the house, re-laid the fire. Made both beds. Fed the cats. Even let them in the house until they irritated her with their grovelling gratitude and she kicked them out again.

The silent feud with Alex had been going on

too long. She got out a bottle of Vitek's Cabernet Sauvignon and looked at it questioningly. She would ring up her sister and invite her around. She would overlook decades of self-exile, several early escapes from – what was the right word? – an adolescence made lonelier because Alex wouldn't confide in her. Yes, she would ask her to lunch. Just Alex. The two of them. She opened the fridge door. There was enough food.

TEN

Norah saw a spider's web quiver. It had hung there unmolested for days, even in the driving rain, spreading its delicate circles under a branch of the magnolia tree, the one that marked the boundary between the two houses.

Alexandra approached in her tan leather shoes – the kind she could buy only at the Strand Arcade – and marched straight through the crystal chandelier, flicking its broken strands off her jacket. A large woman with perfect vision – a useful attribute in an eye-doctor – she was, as usual, preoccupied.

After a glance at the shed to see that no idiot had left the door open Alexandra entered the back way, without knocking, her tread pugnacious, her face oddly red. 'Right then. What have you got to donate, Norah? Any sweaters? Old coats? Scarves? That feathery dress you gave two Christmases ago went down a treat. The old girls fought over it;

feathers went all over the place. Hardly the thing you want in a clinic.' She warded off Norah's smile by fixing her eyes on the bottle of wine. 'You know I don't drink. Can't have trembling hands doing a trachoma op.'

'A coffee then?'

'I'm looking for a jumper I left on the table.' She gazed hard now into Norah's eyes. 'A long red polo-necked jumper that I have only worn twice and which I want to take back to Katoomba Hospital with me.'

'Haven't seen it. Come and have a drink of something.'

'A long red polo-necked jumper that was beside Mum's bed. What's happened to the pendulum on Mother's clock? It's missing.' She stalked past Norah, staking out the territory. This house was hers.

She walked into the kitchen and screamed, 'Someone's let these cats in again. Out! Out!'

Norah eased opened the cork. Perhaps it was premenstrual tension. It seemed to get worse as you got older. But Alex would never mention it. She didn't go in for self-pity.

'You look peaky, Norah. Having another crisis in your love-life? Who is it this time? A poet, a painter, the candle-stick-maker? I suppose you've come home to cry on Daddy's shoulder.' She grinned.

Alex had spent most of her working life in the mobile eye-hospital in various parts of the outback and recently New Guinea. Strange she had gone back to Dad's old battlefields to heal the sick. Now she was on three month's leave, but she was helping out at the local hospital. Bustle, bustle.

Norah could hear her officious tread as she wandered about the house, now in Mum's room, now in Dad's, then in the big guest room she reserved for herself whenever she made a state visit, because it had the biggest and best bed and Alexandra was a big woman who liked to sleep diagonally. Being a widow had certain compensations.

She came back into the kitchen smiling, holding aloft a pale-blue woollen bed-jacket, a bit dowdy and worse for wear.

'Perfect for old Dot. Her tribe comes from up around Darwin and she never stops moaning about the mountain cold. It drives the rest of the patients mad.'

Norah leaped up. 'Give that back, Alex. Give it to me! Now!'

Alexandra stared at her. 'You won't donate a pathetic old bed-jacket to the less fortunate? It's incredible, your selfishness.'

Alexandra held it high, teasing her, dancing around in her wide khaki trousers. Norah still couldn't reach as high. They could have been kids again.

'I have a particular affection for that jacket,' she said, panting and leaping. 'Stop playing games and give it to me.'

'Oh, take your silly bit of tat.' Alexandra threw it at her. 'You're getting like that woman in *Streetcar Named Desire*. Wearing wispy negligees and fussy bed-jackets, what was her name?'

'Blanche Du Bois.'

'Yes, the vain old bag who couldn't face reality.'

Norah folded the bed-jacket with trembling hands and returned it to its rightful place, under the pillow in Mum's old room. Why had Alex been looking under pillows? Proprietorial snooping? Of course she wasn't to know she'd violated a KM fetish.

She hadn't seen Alex for ages and they were already at it. She stared at herself in the long mirror. She certainly looked like an adult, but with Alex it needed confirmation.

'It has sentimental value, you see, Alex,' she said, back in the kitchen. They had knocked over her glass of wine in the struggle, but Alex had already cleaned it up. Now she was sitting opposite, perusing the *Herald*.

'You're looking fit, Alex. Still got that marvellous skin. How do you do it out in the bush?'

Alexandra, munching a biscuit, shrugged, not unpleasantly.

'When are you going back to PNG?'

'Look, Norah. Don't interview me. I get enough of that. Tell me about that daughter of yours. Has she got a job prospect? Don't want her to become a drifter. Or spend her life leeching on a man.'

Norah gulped the wine. 'It's good news about Dad, isn't it? Laurel will cheer him up, spruce him up a bit too.'

'I'd like to give her the once-over. Is she passable? Mum's a hard act to follow.'

'A nice woman. A bit sad. Been manless for years.'

'That's all you ever think about.'

Alexandra began to relax, sprawling at the table. Her clothes were not especially flattering. But she had an eye for materials and the older her clothes got the better they looked. Her bossiness made her enemies in the big hospitals. But in the outback and the jungle she was much loved. Soon she'd be off to PNG again, good. I've always got on her nerves. She thinks I'm a dreamer, the flying hair, someone with a screw loose.

'So everything's okay in dirty old London? Sophie well? Still live in the same flat?'

'Sophie's been driving me nuts.'

'Send her up to New Guinea. We need all the voluntary help we can get.'

Norah sighed. If only. Once she had tried to

lecture Sophie on the merits of taking up medicine like Aunt Alex. Sophie had listened to her, squirming on her chair, then confessed that she had really always wanted to be a fan-dancer.

'I saw a nice shirt on the clothes-line. A new one. Is that the new woman's influence?'

'Yes. She's got taste. With a capital T.'

'But Dad's happiest in an old pair of strides. Letting himself be dressed up like a monkey. He must be in love. Remember when he brought that parachute silk home from New Guinea and told Mum to make it into "drawers for the girls"? Imagine us doing gym at school, standing on our heads, showing our orange silk undies!'

They giggled.

'Remember when all the uncles came round and we danced the hula-hula? What happened to those grass skirts? You can't get them now, you know.' She paused. 'Rufus broke the native boat. It was the only time I ever saw Dad hit him.'

'We were lucky, weren't we, in our parents? When you think what some people have to put up with ... we didn't realise how lucky we were, only noticed the faults; magnified them.'

'Dad made a big mistake selling that Sydney house – before the boom. Right on the water.'

'I'm going to sell *Lyrebird*, you know.'

'You *what*? I didn't believe Justine when she

told me, she's such a fibber. You can't do that, Norah. We promised Mum we'd never sell. She loved both these houses; she made both these gardens out of nothing; we *promised*.'

'But I'm going to have to.' Norah reached over to touch her.

'Don't try to be smarmy with me! You can't get away with that here.'

She leaped up. 'And you've been sleeping in my bed with one of your pickups.'

Norah slumped. Alexandra loomed, thrusting her face angrily down at her. 'You've always been a sneak and a liar.' Her dominant features twisted like a gargoyle's. 'You think you can walk back here whenever you get the urge. Patronising us. Taking things. Mother gave you the house next door because you sucked up to her at the end. Now you're selling it. You don't give a damn. My daughter will be out on her ear. I know you're after the things in this house. Grovelling to Dad. But everything under this roof is *mine*. Understand? Mother left this house to *me*.'

'Of course.' Placate. Placate. Dear Old Sis, she did nothing but good in this naughty world. Underneath Norah felt the old fear rising, the need to run to the edge, merge with the spray.

'I let Dad come and live here when he stupidly sold the Sydney house. Do you think I like him messing up this place so that I have to clean it up when I come home? You're still his favourite. You and Rufus.'

'Rufus is his son.'

'You're as coldblooded as you always were. You just want money. Those poems you used to send home would have made more sense if everywhere you'd written the word "love" you'd crossed it out and put "money" instead. You flatter Dad now, and he purrs. Even when he used to bring home toys for the doll's house ... you got the biggest dressing table, you ...'

The torrent of words splattered up the walls, sloshed about under the divan, scuttled into the cracks between the tiles and even seeped into Grandma's Saratoga trunk in the darkest corner. There was no space left. Her sister's face had grown enormous. It was as it had always been in the beginning. Her sister had got there first. She was bigger and stronger and noisier.

Norah began to feel an ancient lethargy. She sat up stiffly. 'I didn't sleep in your bed with a pickup Alex, I just ...' her voice quivered.

'I know what you just did. In my clean sheets. Whoever he was, he wasn't clean. You leave clues, you see. You know you're not supposed to light a fire in the front room. Dad doesn't like it. You tried to cover it up. I could tell by the typically careless way you'd arranged the kindling.'

Alexandra straddled the doorway. There was no getting away from her. Unless she could reach inward into the dark marrow and find a hiding-place there.

'I had a guest, Alex. I naturally gave him the best room. It's called hospitality. Dad loves me staying here.'

'That is my room. Repeat, *my room*. You do not put strangers in *my* bed.'

Inside the abject sister something turned away. She stood up. She picked up the bottle of Cabernet Sauvignon as if to hurl it.

It was Mother's bed. Mother's nuptial bed. They were fighting over Mother's entrails.

'Piss off, Alex.'

Her sister pushed past her and slammed the porch door. Cats squealed. Norah drank the whole bottle by herself, and merged with the spray.

Sisterhood. Sisters put gravel in your mouth when you're in the pram; plan to separate you from your mother. There was only one thing to do in these embattled times, in this mother-haunted house: have a hot bath.

In the chilly bathroom she unwrapped the bathsalts from all the Christmases of the last quarter century, including the ones she'd missed, some of them gift-packs from London and poured every last one of them into the steaming tub.

Through alps of lather her flesh hit the water with relief. The keen edge of the heat had a sobering effect, of sorts. She lay looking at her peeking toes, making lists of lovers to the smell of Rose and Fern, picking up handfuls of foam and blowing fluffy bits towards the window where they separated into bubbles, each launching a tiny rainbow. She slithered in suds for ages, topping up the water when it got too cold, slurping more wine from the bottle.

If KM had been her sister, she would sit there on the edge of the bath in an embroidered kimono and they would have had a good old-fashioned gossip.

What was the dentist like in bed?

It wasn't in bed, but on the forest floor.

What about the ants?

You forget, I was dying. We rented a room in the village, but it was too sordid, with oil stains on the wall above the sagging bed, so we fled back to the forest.

No wonder you died of TB.

He was the best cure for all my ills.

None of your biographers got onto it, did they? But I did because you failed to describe the long walk into that forest in your usual plangent detail. I found that suspicious.

You live vicariously. I find that sad.

Why shouldn't I write a biographical radio drama about you?

Biography is a hyena of an art, feeding on leftovers, mixing up bones.

There was a violent crashing overhead. Norah sat up, trembling, foam sliding down her back. Must be possums having a territorial fight on the roof. It sounded like dozens of them. The corrugated iron could cave in and instead of K she'd have a bloody great possum in her bath. That sobered her up.

ELEVEN

Norah heard the delivery boy walk up the drive.

'Who's that sitting on her own in the garden?'

'The old man's other daughter. Over from England. Got a hangover,' said Andy, resting on his spade, studying the paper boy's face. Only last year it was a clear young face; this year there was corruption in it.

'I know the perfect cure.' He winked.

Andy put down his spade. 'You should come down to the park. I'll teach you to row on the lake.'

Too right, Norah thought. He would stand behind him, yes, breathing heavily on his neck, the fine hairs on the nape parting, then he'd run a hand down his arm resting it paternally on his fist. 'Hold the oar like this,' he'd say, watching his crotch for signs of life.

The boy kicked out at Andy, dislodging a

zinnia. 'Dirty old perv. You're a health hazard.'

To take her mind off her hangover, Norah undid the straps around Grandma's Saratoga trunk. It was stuffed with photographs and family documents of one kind and another. Rummaging about inside as if drawing a winning raffle ticket her hand closed over a journal, bound so tightly with tapes that the dust had got into the knot. She worked it loose with a kebab skewer, smelling a stale whiff of 'Evening in Paris', Mother's scent. It was written in Mother's jagged handwriting. With a voyeur's guilt she peeped at a few entries, holding the journal at some distance, half afraid, half sad. Mother never had a single evening in Paris in her life; so she had to make do with the scent; that indigo blue bottle on her dressing table, the colour of endlessly imagined starry nights over the Seine.

Love at first sight is love at second sight. Balzac said that. You, my bit of flotsam from Europe, have Balzac in your blood. But you are behaving like a larrikin. Rushing in to eat, borrow books, rushing off again.

Are you embarrassed by my age? I've just plucked out another grey hair. Ah, but Adonis, I have kissed your boyish chest which contains, I know, the shards of a heart, the bits that weren't blown up in the Warsaw tram. Sshh, we won't speak about that again. I made that promise in the hut when you covered me from head to foot with boronia blossom. There was no embarrassment then, was there with you, naked, playing your violin for me, my troubadour.

I feel ghastly. I shouldn't have, but I did. I phoned you. How calm and cool my voice sounded. You said, I've been thinking about you. You were trying to throw me bouquets. Oh, what a fool am I! I want to hurl myself off the cliff. But the children condemn me to life.

I think I heard my heart break. I phoned you, and some whore was laughing in the background. You swine. You haven't contacted me for two weeks. You're with some piece of damaged goods. You've drained me of everything. What do you give me in return? Cocky gander with his geese and crooked with it.

Norah came home late again looking cheap. I slapped her face. Just the way my odious mother used to slap mine. We try to get rid of the monster mother in us but she's always there.

Norah looked out over the garden. The zinnias, sweetpeas, hydrangeas. That's where it had all ended up, all that rush of blood. It had gone underground and re-emerged years later in herbacious borders.

She went down to the incinerator, lit the fire, and fed it with Mother's secret journal. Flames into flames. As she stood there staring, a little dried seahorse slipped out from between the pages and flared up for one instant; a phoenix.

Ah, yes, she remembered the softness of the night air as she'd come home, up the verandah and into the hard brightness of the kitchen. Mother had been scribbling in her journal and chain smoking. She saw my great translucent eyes, my pouting pubescent lips and slapped me, right across the mouth. All my gleaming tumescence crumpled into outrage and tears. It was the first push out of the nest, out of Mother's hair.

Norah's headache had gone; she was free of it. And she had urgent news for Vitek. She had to tell him instantly. Now. Before another thousand years rushed by. Had to spit it out: tell him, yes, that she loved him.

The nearest public box was down by the railway station. She shot back into the house for her purse and straight out the front door again, running all the way down past the whizzing avenue of eucalyptuses, grey-green colanders of dripping sunlight; past the trucks roaring along the Great Western Highway; past the amused locals. Inside the phone box she was safe from eavesdroppers, although closely observed by a line of Rosellas on the station fence.

She had long ago vowed never to ring lovers at their workplace; never to be one of that despised legion of pestering amorous females.

She dialled his office number.

The pert young voice of his secretary answered. 'I'll see if Mr Vic is available.'

He's sitting there in his eyrie. He'll talk. He's got to. I'm part of his history, for Godsake. Without me he'd be dead; bones whitened by the sea. Oh, come on. Put him through. Put him through. Without him I wouldn't have a daughter to worry about. I wouldn't know what love was.

'Sorry. Mr Vic is tied up in a meeting.'

The telephone sagged like the freckly arm that supported it.

She walked slowly back, pushing against the press of the returning headache. Tied up in a meeting, eh? Instructing brokers to shift huge sums of money about? Haranguing the underlings? Or screwing his latest lunch date? No, it wouldn't be that because the secretary was in the annexe.

As Norah toiled up the long hill homeward, a more convincing possibility presented itself. Yes, she saw him clearly, the president of Vic Enterprises, sitting there in his thirty-eighth floor suite breathing into a brown paper bag. In out, in out, forcing himself to remain calm and watch the bag swell and deflate until his breathing returned to normal. If the strain of being a tycoon had to manifest itself, let it be in hyperventilation rather than tumours or impotence. At least he'd stopped wetting the bed.

It must have been Mother who had cured him of that. Not by some kind of conscious therapy, just by taking him on; mothering him in the way she had never mothered Norah. In return he must have worked on her body with the extra zeal of gratitude.

When the paper bag expanded it would hide the Lautrec lithograph. When it contracted he would see the two figures in bed, just tousled heads on pillows. Even their genders are ambiguous. The blankets and sheets, a few authoritative strokes, reach up to their chins. They gaze eternally at each other with a look both sated and untrusting.

Yes, Vitek, breathing in and out, on Hayman Island with Mother. The hairy tarantulas on the cabin walls, the door wide open, the sea roaring at him to get up and out into its exploding blues, the morning air fizzing with possibilities. He pulls on his shorts and runs out to the beach and sees her in the distance crouching over a wriggling crescent of turtles, turning them on their bellies so they can shamble back to the sea.

After that island holiday he never smelled of piss again.

Mother had been this happy only once

before, for a few years after leaving school, before her father died of tetanus poisoning. Then she had married the first man to propose. She was terrified of becoming one of those sad old maids that littered the world then, yellowing and wispy as brown leaves, turning nasty or potty: unsung casualties from the First World War. Dad had been so gorgeous. Like a movie star. It was Mother who had made the first move, tickling his feet with a blade of grass. Frisky, girlish fun. Then came the three children and boredom.

But then her young Polish lover, the only lover she had ever had, became conceited. Every woman and girl in the land loved a Polish violinist. Especially if they could be a bit sorry for him, starving in his hostel.

When Norah grabbed him in the pool that time (saved him from drowning in all senses), he hadn't known his power over Australian women, usually treated like mothers by their husbands or cowered from in mock terror as cartoon shrews if they asserted themselves.

There must have been something novel and exhilarating in Mother's eye. Norah shuddered. She saw him reach out to touch her mother's breast for the first time, relieved that it did not sag; her face flamed.

But hadn't she been the same? Following him everywhere, her cow-eyes mooing at him, her thin colt legs tightening around him, making him struggle to be free.

Norah arrived exhausted at her front gate. By now Vitek's panic attack would have subsided. He would not want to take on more responsibilities. It must be hard to believe in a child that cast no shadow before it; that cost nothing. No babyhood, no childhood, no compost of memories. Now to be presented with a fully-grown daughter, springing from his head like Minerva! Why should he believe in it? He had cut her and Sophie out of his mind. Now she would cut him out of her mind. But she allowed him a parting flourish – she saw him, with one clap of his hand, bursting the paper bag and summoning his secretary who entered, in cute alarm.

TWELVE

Dad came out of the train wearing a new pale blue tropical jacket and a carnation in his buttonhole.

'Flash as a rat with a gold tooth,' observed the station master.

Driving him up the hill Norah said, 'I'm afraid I had a row with Alex.'

'You girls. Always fighting. It drove your mother mad.'

'How was Sydney?'

'Hot. It's nicer up here. But Laurel doesn't like it. Says it's full of your mother, and Alex tracking her every move in case she appropriates something.'

'Alex complained that the pendulum of the clock was missing.'

He let out an exasperated sigh. 'I took it off. Couldn't stand the bloody ping. She doesn't miss a trick. There's just too much surveillance. I have more privacy at Laurel's.'

When they parked at the garage, Dad stood behind the Holden waving her back in to the garage. She reversed slowly so she wouldn't knock the sides off the door, watching him through the rear-vision mirror. Suddenly he shouted, 'You've put that damned suitcase in my garage. Get it out!'

She applied the handbrake with a clenched fist.

He was still going on about it when she came out and rolled down the garage door. 'I'm not storing that man's trunk. Get rid of it today!'

In a few days she would be leaving the country. In some ways she wouldn't be sorry. Family was a Gordian knot. It felt tighter, more real, more final than any other bonds she'd ever struggled in. But she sometimes suspected that whenever she got tangled up with a man, it was the moment of breaking free she really enjoyed.

'You keep away from bad types, dear. When you were seventeen, I saw you with one boy on the bus, another on the ferry and a third on the tram, all when I was on my way home one evening from the office. There's no doubt about it, it's in the family blood.'

Norah smiled at her giddy years. When Vitek was around, she had produced so much pollen that boys came out of the sky; they fell like rain.

Dad fumbled at the lock. She could have

opened it quicker, but he wouldn't budge until he'd mastered it. She followed his huge bent body up the hall. 'Oh and that Vozzek cove, I ran into him at the bank. He asked me about my medals. Decent cove that. Why didn't you marry him?'

'A good question, Dad.'

'He asked after you. Seemed concerned. You'll be hearing from him, mark my words. He was taking out wads of money. A good catch that one.'

Her sad old barnacled heart gave a tiny lurch, like a beast not quite dead.

'How about buying a ticket for the ball?' asked the butcher. His walls were covered with pictures of trotting horses and Princess Diana. They all had a sleek equestrian shine.

'I'll buy some raffle tickets instead.'

She avoided looking at the meat: slippery liver, red-veined brains and hearts with tubes attached. What a hypocrite she was, queasy at the butcher's and a meat guzzler at the barbies. Behind her stood the novelist with the bird's nest hairdo. She bottled her own wine, presenting samples to the locals which invariably exploded months later in their sheds. The novelist inquired after Dad with peculiar intensity, adjusting her hair combs. She was his reserve squad in case Laurel fell in action. Next in line stood the dentist's wife whose voice was as piercing as her husband's drill.

'They're shooting all the dingoes round Ayers Rock, looking for the remains of that baby. They should do the same to those lying cheating parents; hang their flamin' skins on the dingo fence.'

'You never know,' said the butcher, chopping the bone off a shoulder of lamb, twisting it back, rolling the joint in paper. 'Never can tell till it's proved.'

'There was blood all over the car. Now, is it natural to have a blood-soaked car if you're a parson? Doesn't that strike you as odd?' drilled the dentist's wife.

'You've got a point there,' said the butcher.

He had a lynch mob on his hands. But they were the same people who came out to fight the fires, sometimes working all through the night with hoses and axes. No one got paid. And it didn't matter whose land it was.

As a youth the butcher used to clean out the stables at her old boarding school. He had seen them, at bell-clanging dawn, running on the double to the flag pole to sing 'Rule Britannia' and the rest of the canon. He had seen them learning 'How India Became British', 'How Canada Became British', 'How South Africa Became British', 'How

161

Australia Became British', in that order, from the old history books. He'd been there hauling in the sludge when they'd painted pine cones patriotic colours, using ink for the red and blue and tennis-shoe liquid for the white. Like all bullies the head-mistress had been unpredictable. The girls had thought the painted cones would give her pleasure, feed her obsession for Empire, but for their initia-tive they had been beaten on the shins with a coathanger.

Andy came shambling into the shop and stood too close to the women. The butcher looked up sharply. Andy was everybody's problem, like the fires. Why Norah's father hired this nasty piece of work to do the garden was a bit of a puzzle.

'What do you want, Andy?'

'Gotter bita news. It's going round the pubs.'

'Yeah?'

'Another bloke died down in the valley.'

'Hiker?'

'Nah. Worked for the council. Remember the last bloke was drowned in them flash floods last November? Well, they found this bloke early this morning. He'd fallen over the edge near the Vic-toria Pass. Silly bugger. Overloaded. Face all blis-tered. Skinny as a whippet. Had a funny name. Peter Duck.'

The raffle tickets fluttered out of Norah's hand.

She couldn't cry, but there was a tightness in her chest as she drove unsteadily home. At least they had had the mushroom day. A free box for nothing. If life was a movie she would have slept with him in the magic valley, after all that released emotion, leaving behind broken stalks and the reek of fungus. Perhaps there had been something about Pete that had reminded her of Vitek before he became fat and successful.

She sighed. It was the inevitable backwash after any death. You just wished you'd paid more attention. Maybe that night's shelter at the big old house had meant something to a man who slept rough.

The day had settled to its thickest heat. Even through the sealed car you could hear the locust din. It was that time of the day: monotonous, dangerous, before the exploding of tempers, before the wind comes up. She got out to open the roller-door of the garage. Dad had left Pete's suitcase rather pointedly outside on the gravel. She opened the lid. A smell of old socks assailed her. There was a coiled up plastic belt, a couple of dirty magazines – his family heirlooms. She shut the lid and threw the case into the boot. She would have to take it to the dump.

THIRTEEN

There was an urgent message waiting for her from Vitek. Could she meet him that evening just before sunset at the bottom of Victoria Street in the Cross.

Dad passed it on with a knowing lilt in his voice. 'There's a proposal coming up. I warned you. I used to like to sit with your mother on Lady Macquarie's Chair at that time of day.'

'Dad! He's not divorced yet.' But she begged him for the car so she could leave immediately. 'What time is sunset?' she asked, then regretted it as he fumbled slowly with the newspapers, searching in vain for the weather charts.

'I mean, approximately . . .'

'You're the one always going up to Pulpit Rock to watch the sun go down. You should know.'

Of course. She hit her forehead. She knew. But her brain had seized up.

All the way down she listened to pops on

the car radio, singing along with her favourites – 'When you're in love with a beautiful woman'. She whizzed round the corner at Medlow Bath like a racing driver. Oh, love, love, love, all the songs were about love. All that money he had drawn from the bank. Was it for her? Had he understood? Yes. He had realised that she was too embarrassed to ask him for money and that her, *their*, daughter's clinic must be out of her league financially. Usually Australian men were huffy with her. Their eyes, the way they glazed with distrust, made her awkward and nervous. It was Vitek's Polishness that had first attracted her. His Polish Jewish blood. Darker, marinated in depth.

She roared down on to the plains and speeded up. She was summoned, summoned at last, *claimed*. Neither his bulk nor his baldness mattered. When two people met in their youth that's the way they saw each other for ever. His youthful characteristics were imprinted on your mind with every detail intact: one shoulder slightly lower than the other, and that brown mole on the jawline. He was always that hairy foreigner she had first met in the pool. Love really was eternal after all. Silly her, she had fallen into her old gloomy habits. Once she had been the opposite, sensing a Godly presence, the sweetness and the power. Now Sophie might be claimed too. The return of the Father. The full orchestration of fulfilment.

'How Deep is Your Love?' she sang as she swept by the dull and penurious western suburbs where stout women in track suits gazed sullenly at her as at a shooting star.

It had been twenty-five years, not so long, if you thought about it. Time was speeding up anyhow. Just twenty-five turns of the wheel. They were playing 'Fascinating Rhythm', her mother's era but another song she had not liked:

When a highbrow meets a lowbrow
Going down old Broadway
Soon that highbrow he's got no brow
Oh what a shame, you are to blame ...

She got stuck behind two semi-trailers, but the radio played Tina Turner. Mother would have actively disliked Tina Turner, much as she disliked Sophie's heavy metal. Divergent pop music was the necessary lever that disconnected the generations.

She glanced at her face in the driving mirror. Makeup was just a marginal help. Beauty came from the soul and that was that. Perhaps she was in a manic state now. If she was, the swing to depression would arrive all too soon and last six times as long. But the thought of that future bucket of water wasn't enough to douse the flames.

She was early of course. So she wandered about Victoria Street admiring the houses, each with its own follies and fancies. A derelict woman staggered across the road and begged for money.

She hurried past with averted eyes, but then returned and the woman snatched her dollars without meeting her eye. Everyone hates having to ask for money. She thought of foisting Pete's suitcase on her. It was a nuisance rolling about in the boot and there might be something in it she could sell, but better not, she might feel insulted.

By the time Vitek's car came cruising by she had quietened down. But her fingers were trembling and her palms were moist.

'Hop in, Norah. I've got to find a parking place.'

'You park. I'll catch up with you.' Physical closeness was too much just yet. She had to take a few deep breaths to calm herself.

She kept several yards away from him as they walked into the courtyard of a block of flats. 'What's this, a mystery tour?'

He smiled.

She stood at the far side of the lift imagining them both naked in the lift. Now that would be about as naked as you could get.

They went down a short hall and he produced a key, unlocked a door, held it open for her. She entered and stood there unmoving. The harbour wrapped itself around the long curved window; it was like being on the prow of a ship. The whole Sydney razzamatazz was out there: the Bridge, the Opera House, the sailing boats, the catamarans and, for added effect, the incoming drama of a Russian tanker, *Alexandre Pushkin*.

'It's marvellous.'

'It's for you.'

'Me?'

'You and me.'

She prowled around the room. It seemed to be all anyone would ever need in a room, with a kitchen adjoining and the only door leading into a bathroom which overlooked the Botanical Gardens. You could never feel claustrophobic here; even though it was only one room.

'For you and me,' she repeated. 'But there is only one room.'

'I could come after work. At least two days a week.'

As Norah leant against the wall, she could feel herself deflate. Couldn't he hear the hiss of expiring steam?

'Oh, I see. A love nest.'

'You could leave London and live in it. You know. For the rest of the time.'

'Oh. Thanks.'

'Look, I'm offering you a flat.'

'With one room.'

'Look at the view. Think of the future.'

'Where's Sophie going to sleep?'

Vitek took off his coat and hung it on the chair. He loosened his tie, opened the fridge and took out a bottle of chilled champagne. He handed her the drink with a roguish gesture; a seducer in a Marx Brother movie.

The cork popped and champagne spurted on the ceiling. 'That won't be the only thing spurting on the ceiling,' he said.

'I see. You plan to practise onanism.'

'You're not as pretty as my wife. But you suit me in other ways.'

'Perhaps you could put us both in the blender and create the perfect woman.'

'Take your clothes off.'

'I'll say one thing for you, Vitek,' she said wearily, disrobing, 'you don't do a very elaborate mating dance.'

'It's been over twenty years; that's enough mating dance.'

'No, it hasn't.' She kicked off her tights. 'It's been five minutes.'

He poured champagne on her breasts. She cradled his head thinking of something she'd read once, that old ladies in the Third World give suck to starving infants. Her breasts tightened. Of course he couldn't take the thought of his daughter seriously. He'd never met her. How can you love an abstraction? She craned her neck at his watch while he got to work. She would drive straight back. Didn't want to come in too late and disturb Dad. He would rush out with the Samurai sword. Vitek would just have to keep this place for the next girl. God knows, there must be legions of them.

He moved upon her now as if she wasn't making other plans. Soon she got involved. The room was rocking. The harbour poured into her eyes, furrowed in light. Her breasts ballooned, white and voluptuous as the Opera House. His back arched over her like the Bridge. A seagull skidded against the window; she saw its startled black eye, its flustered grab at the glass, but she was too pre-occupied to decide whether it was a good omen. At the critical moment *Alexandre Pushkin* boomed three times. They both laughed.

'Hope I wasn't too heavy.'

'I like roly-poly men. It was my favourite nursery song: "Roly poly gammon and spinach hey ho says Anthony Roley." '

'I can fix you up with a job in broadcasting. No sweat.'

'You're sweating like the great sweltering wheeler dealer you are, my love.'

He laughed. 'I spoke to Mike Colowsky. I told him you were personable; bright. You knew how to read and write.' Vitek gave a satisfied, fixer's chuckle. 'He says you can work on the News Desk. Good pay. You'll pick it up fast. We'll have lots of fun.'

'Ah, fun.'

'What's wrong with fun?'

'Nothing. I think fun is very deep stuff.'

She stood up telling herself to shut up but saying it anyhow. 'You forget one thing. *Sophie.* Where will she sleep?'

Vitek prowled his domain. He loved Sydney. Australia. More than she did. Loved what it had given him. 'Ah, come on, Norah. She's grown up. At least she would be if you stopped fussing over her and started treating her like an adult. People have to sink or swim.'

She stared at him. He is drowning – the big wave washing over the rocks swirls him off to crash on the roof, splintering into a thousand points of light; a black diamond that was once a piece of Poland. Then her own skinny sixteen-year-old arm reaches out and grabs him.

'After all,' he said, 'you and I made it on our own. She'll decide when she's had enough self-pun-ishment. Then she'll come out of it. You wait. You'll see. She'll just stop. Especially if *you* stop wringing your hands and get on with your own life. Being a drug addict is like that classic adolescent fantasy of being present at your own funeral. I mean where's the fun in destroying yourself if no one mourns. Everything you do just stops her growing up.'

She looked at him carefully. Men didn't understand about mother love. How it is stronger even than passion, stronger than empires, stronger than *them*. But her habit of boosting men was so ingrained that she didn't tell him to fuck off there and then. She laughed and gossiped a bit and made promises of future meetings. Tomorrow she would write him the truth, and post it, pure in heart, cold as a bureaucrat clearing a desk.

Before they left, they went around closing the windows, picking up the bits and pieces of paper blown about by the sea breezes.

They both saw it at the same time, lying in the very centre of the desk. A dead seagull. It must have flown in while they were screwing. Came in to die. They stared at the cadaver and shuddered.

FOURTEEN

The juniper tree was in fruit. Bones were buried under them in fairytales, but the tree always squealed in the end. The old pine bent at an angle of more than forty-five degrees would collapse in the next wind-storm. That's what everyone had been saying for years, but it still held up despite its many hollows, Alexandra's favourite hiding place for the Easter eggs.

Now all this domain would be her sister's. She wouldn't be part of it. Alexandra had won somehow. Her mother's kingdom. Some stranger would buy her house next door. Someone who wouldn't count.

She got into the car. In her folder she had the documents from the house agent. She also had to confirm her flight to London. And buy some crates of beer for the farewell party.

Through the car window the morning air had never been sweeter, but it was going to be too windy.

Every time she turned the hairpin bends, Pete's suit-case rolled in the boot, and the wind tried to push her off the road. Empty bottles rattled. She had planned to redecorate *Lyrebird*, knock a wall down between the kitchen and living room; settle there one day with a couple of dogs and who knew who else? It had given her strength, knowing *Lyrebird* was waiting there, a sense of acres of pine forests in her blood, even as she had sat gloomily in the London tube, stalled between stops on the Northern Line. She had lain awake on the other side of the world wondering if a willow would grow at this altitude, knowing a jacaranda wouldn't, planning to grow more wisteria around the back and to move the unsightly clothes-line behind the rho-dodendrons. It was like holding a rosary; telling the beads.

She came to the turn-off for the dump. The old Holden had to be driven slowly over the dust. As she approached, the smell assaulted her; dis-carded newspapers blew about, wingless vultures; desolation angels.

She parked on the clay edge. Scroungers were picking over the remains of a rusty pusher. The child had found a skate with a broken strap, his face stern and dusty as he inspected the rusty wheels.

She watched them warily. Alone in the bush she was seldom scared, but alone in a dump except for derelicts – maybe she had watched too much lousy TV. They toiled on, glum and determined.

Perhaps they were frightened of her. Perhaps they thought she had bits of a baby in that disgusting old suitcase she was hauling out of the boot.

She threw the old can on the pile but tripped on a legless doll in the slime and the faulty catch sprang the lid wide open. Filthy socks flew on to the clay. All that was left of that sweet man. One of his dirty magazines was snatched by a gust of wind. The boy put down his skate and chased after the picture of a huge pair of buttocks and a girl's simper.

She plodded back to the car and got the crate of empty wine bottles.

She had been drinking too much. Not getting on with her work. In the wing mirror she caught a glimpse of her face. Her looks were going. Death moved so slowly. He was such an expert lover. First the touch under the eyes, then the move down to the throat; no doubt the breasts would go next. She swung the crate on to the rubbish; it landed on top of the case which now toppled right over, releasing an old Arnott's biscuit tin from under a pair of trousers. As it slid further down the pile of refuse, its lid opened. Out rolled an exquisite white cup.

She stared at the miracle in the slime. Not even Mother's best china could compare. Shaped in the form of a white rose on a gold stem, it wove sunlight from its scalloped curves. Magpies gathered around like Mafia extortionists in their undertaker suits. She moved in closer and rummaged in the tin.

There were no more of the wondrous cups, but she drew out two old photographs in silver frames and a set of elaborate silver salt cellars, with hallmarks and dates: 1772, 1873 and one very faint date which could be 1674. The frames were edged with filigree and sported a family crest. Silver flashed in the sun, light into light.

Inside the broken glass there was a photograph of an Edwardian lady holding the rose cup, the chalice fit for Venus. In the background stood the maid. It was Peter Duck in a frilly cap. Same pinched features. Same oddly velvety eyes. At once she felt a rush of wild surmise.

In the other photograph the hostess stood on the steps of a white colonial house, her arms around a girl. The girl was plump and frizzy-haired, no resemblance to her svelte familiar Mansfield. But the eyes had the weight in them of impending genius.

At last, at the bottom of the tin she found a bundle of old letters, bound together with a single embroidered garter. She looked behind her with the scared look of a hyena who had been left the kill, too overwhelmed to unfold the letters in case she damaged them. But she read a few lines:

... half mad with love. Do not let custom hedge you in. I have swept away all my recollections of Caesar and Adonis, all that terrible banality. Remember only our swim, our night ...

With shaking hands she packed Pete's heirlooms back inside the tin. Her dress got soaked with the slime of a rotting cabbage. A rubber tyre slid slowly down the incline. She tried to think. KM sitting on top of an abandoned fridge was kicking her legs, showing off the other matching garter. One little mule hung by its toe. And she was laughing her raucous colonial arpeggio.

Were these the missing love letters to that old lady who said they'd been burnt? The writing seemed familiar. The delicate sketches. But the signature was an indecipherable squiggle. Had Pete's gran stolen them to do a spot of blackmail? Was this a literary coup? Fallen into her hands by wild miraculous serendipity?

She stood up, shaking out her skirt. No. This was too fantastic.

Her enchantress was still sitting there on the rotting fridge adjusting her phantom mule. What firm brown feet she had. What a teasing smile. How real unreality was. Like any vision in any grotto seen from an obsessed mind.

Of course they wouldn't be Mansfield's letters. Someone else's from the same period. Of no interest to fans or biographers or the British Museum or rich American collectors.

'Hey, Miss!' Norah turned and saw the boy with the broken skate still dangling from his hand. He had a crooked gambler's grin. 'I'll swop you the skate

for one of them silver things you was chucking out.'
He peered at her. Just how mad was this woman in
the clay? Most of the scroungers were nuts. 'You can
keep the photers. Just one lousy bit of silver. You
never know, you might find the other skate.'

The boy knew the substance from the
shadow. It was the silver that was valuable, if anything. The rest was just wishful thinking, her
wanted miracle and, of course, deliverance for
Sophie from the evil spell.

'Here, you can have the cup,' she said, pla-
cating the gods, handing him something she really
wanted for herself.

'But it's cracked.' He went off to show it to
his soiled parents who didn't believe in their luck,
and would get a surprise at just how much the old
cup fetched.

The cemetery was on the highway lined with
half-grown Japanese cherries. She parked at the
gate and, carrying a potted chrysanthemum, walked
through the Catholic section to her mother's grave.
A camellia had already been planted behind the
headstone. Alex always got in first with expressions
of love. Or was that just her own jealousy writhing
away? There was a jar of withered tulips on the
gravel, toppled by wind.

She straightened it up, letting the gravel slide through her fingers. There was no space for her next to the grave, that was already taken by the butcher's mother. Just as well. Alex would claim it. Nothing would ever change between them in that direction. Best to stay on the other side of the world. She put down the chrysanthemum, wedging it stable with stones. The next wind would blow it down.

She sat there for a while, the palms of her hands pressing on the grave and felt a deep slow warmth work its way through her whole being. A love transfusion.

'Pete.' She said his name out loud, causing a man walking by with a horse to look back. Pleasure at her good fortune swept over the windy universe. The trees bent double under the weight of it. Like the two brown eagles soaring up above, she saw all obstacles shrink below her. What had been huge mountains before became mere bumps on a gradient map. That silver was sufficiently valuable (maybe Georgian or earlier), without taking into account the letters.

She stood up and walked back briskly to the car. On the strength of it she would cancel the sale of her house.

FIFTEEN

Rufus came up early with some wines and dumped it all on the kitchen table. He still felt embarrassed and angry with Norah who was hovering about straightening tea towels. They hadn't looked crooked to him. He took down a glass and polished it zealously, then poured himself a beer.

Andy was nosing around the back door for his tea and biscuits. So much was going on he'd been forgotten. Norah put on the kettle. Got out his tray. If she hurried, perhaps he wouldn't come in.

'He gives me the creeps.'

'Oh, poor old Andy. You're too hard, Norah.'

'Why do we keep him on? He just pretends to garden. He hasn't got the energy to turn the turf. And he hasn't got the mind of a gardener. Mind of a sewer.'

'Well you know, he was Dad's batman in the war.'

'So what?'

180

'Poor old Andy.'

Dad entered the kitchen and let Andy in. 'At ease, Corporal. Tea's up,' he said.

Andy sat at the table. His pervert's eyes slid over the middle-aged children. Rufus first, then, less enthusiastically, Norah.

'Clipped those hedges, have you, Andy? Didn't like the look of them last time.'

'Pruned them blackberries,' he said, dunking a biscuit in tea so hot that the biscuit at once collapsed and drowned in its own squelchiness.

Dad offered him another biscuit, closed the lid, replaced the tin, straightened up. In the ensuing silence he pretended to be interested in the train timetables.

'What's the drill, Andy? What time do you clock-off today?'

Andy cautiously dunked his second biscuit but scalded his fingertips. 'Remember that bloke, the screwball, useter pour paraffin on some of the men and set light to them?'

Relieved, Dad sat down. Recycling old stories was a social relief, especially the good ones, polished to perfection like the glass in Rufus's hands.

'The whole battalion was terrified.' Dad chuckled.

'You woke up one night ...' Andy prompted.

'I heard someone breathing under my stretcher ...'

Norah sliced celery and frayed the edges; she couldn't remember this story.

'Yes, I could hear a man breathing loudly. It was pitch dark in the tent.'

'What did you do? Norah said.

'Just lay there. Didn't move a muscle.'

They all laughed. Except Andy.

'Best thing you could've done, Sir.'

'Just lay there. Too frightened to breathe.'

Norah put the celery in ice cubes. 'Then what happened, Dad?'

'A dark shape emerged and ran for the tent opening. I yelled and ... well ... carry on, Corporal ... '

'Right, Sir. Well, I was ready for him. I threw paraffin at him, and then I threw a lighted match. Gave the bastard a taste of his own medicine.' Andy laughed, scattering crumbs into a curious knotted silence.

Dad stood up. 'You should have got promoted. That swine's been in an asylum ever since.'

'He survived?' Norah whispered.

'Oh, yes. We were billeted on a beach. He jumped in the ocean. Andy showed great presence of mind.'

Andy beamed. For once his eyes stopped their swivelling. In wartime you did bad things and they praised you. He wished it was that time again.

Alexandra stood in the kitchen mixing cream cheese and chives. It had always been like this. Norah curled up with some poetry anthology, eyes huge with Keats while Alexandra cleaned the brass and scrubbed the floors. Norah's very earliest memory was of Alex standing on a chair with a tea towel round her waist beating up batter with a wooden spoon when Mum started smashing dirty dishes against the wall. All of a sudden. It was Mum who should have been the one curled up reading Keats. She wasn't cut out to be a housewife. That was why she had encouraged Norah to go overseas the minute she left school. Norah had done her travelling for her. And Mum had admired her for it.

Norah and Rufus were still lazing about in the garden and people were due any minute. Norah could hear her sister thumping about in the kitchen. She probably resented her for not pulling her weight on the domestic front. But so what, tomorrow night she'd be off again to London.

The night was sharp. But mist was imminent.

It would be a pearly one, fine as ectoplasm; not like those sinister old London peasoupers. Soon after Norah had arrived in London, her feet frozen from the lack of snow boots, she had looked out of a cafe window into the heart of the fog and seen a blind beggar appearing and disappearing through the engulfing greyness. This apparition from the depths of the mystery that was London had piped a dirge. Another stunted figure had pushed the blind piper through the fog, while beating a death march on a tin drum. A hallucination perhaps, caused by cold and loneliness.

Inside the big house the family party was brewing. But the stars held her outside. In London she had been star-starved. She would like to lie down now on the moist lawn and gaze up at them until they dropped, each one a jewel you could wrap in silk; negotiable one day ... Oh God, now she was starting to think like KM, a creeping form of plagiarism was setting in.

Behind her a door opened, footsteps approached in a ray of light.

'The moths are bad tonight.' Alex was holding drinks and a few peanuts in a napkin.

In the dark it was easier to make up after the last row. Somewhere a dog barked. It came from miles away but it sounded so close, and over the eastern precipices came the wail of the Katoomba Express.

'Mother used to nag Dad for years to get fly

screens.' Norah flipped up a nut and failed to catch it in her mouth. 'Let's toast the girl who burnt down the old school.'

'What we went through. Another century. Like the school in *Jane Eyre*. The Victorian era survived much longer out here.'

'One day it will all be revealed. The scandal of the sadistic headmistress.'

'Do you remember that time, you know, Norah, when we tried to have a pillow fight in the dorm and we heard that old bitch approaching? Everyone leaped back into bed, in their billowing flannel nighties. But you ...'

'I did my breathing exercises.'

'You stood there solemnly, with your arms raised, breathing in and breathing out by the window. You always were a good actress.'

'You should talk. You sank to your knees, pretending to say your prayers. Hypocrite!'

'Well, we escaped a beating that time.'

The door banged open again. 'Come inside, girls. We're going to have a sing-song soon.'

'Half a minute, Uncle.'

'Don't be long, dear.' The door banged shut.

'Has he brought his ukulele?'

'Of course.'

'Justine's so relieved you've decided not to pitch her out and sell your house. It's a great place to bring up kids.'

'Why doesn't she live here in this house? After all, you own it.'

'Justine couldn't live with Dad. Who could?'

'Laurel, apparently.'

'I think she's responsible for the disappearance of the pendulum on Mum's clock. Those elegant, powdered ladies are always the ones who shop-lift. I suppose every time it pings it reminds her of Mum.'

Her words covered the darkness like the words on the Angostura bottle, invading the deeper dark of the gorge and softening the edges of the night until there were no spaces left for the bogies to enter. Under all the bombast Alex was still the child afraid of the dark.

'I wonder who the anarchist was who crapped in the wash basin, in our dormitory. What a stink.'

Alex laughed, heartily, slapping her knee. 'That was me. Didn't you know?'

For a moment silence rushed back to fill the gorge that lay below them and between them.

'But the entire dormitory was punished!' Norah wanted to hit her.

'Oh, by the way, I hear you're a bit short of money.'

Norah blushed in the dark. 'If you're worried about me getting money out of Dad I haven't even asked. And Rufus has his usual cash-flow problem.'

She wouldn't make any announcement about what she'd found in the dump, just in case it turned out to be all moonshine.

'I thought you had a sound career in broadcasting.'

'A wobbly career. Everything's wobbly now, even the unsinkable BBC.'

'Ah.' Alex spread her legs, taking up most of the bench. Tonight she had made a gesture towards the party by wearing black velvet trousers, but they were still cut too wide. 'Work is the secret of life you know, not sex.'

Norah stared up at the unfathomable stars. They knew that the secret of life was life. Then she felt a hand touch hers.

'I can give you five thousand dollars or so,' Alex said. 'How much do you want?'

Norah breathed in. Maybe this sweet and tender mountain air really had cured her lungs.

Norah went through the house with a box of matches lighting everything that could be lit. Dusty kindling sprung uneasily into flame, while Dad grumbled about the danger of setting fire to the chimneys.

She lit all the red candles and even put one in the piano's last remaining gilt candelabra. She couldn't remember anyone doing that before.

Alex peered at the sheet-music by its flickering light, getting ready to pound away at all the old favourites. The uncle with the ukulele turned on the lamp. It might be Norah's farewell party, but she carried the romance stuff too far.

Justine came over to Norah and sat on the ground at her feet, displaying long lace-up bondage boots. 'Want a joint. Auntie Norah?'

'Nope. Where's your baby tonight? She doesn't want a stoned mother.'

'Live for the moment. We're all going to be blown away any minute now.'

'Rubbish.'

'Well, where does your romantic bullshit get you?'

'I've been thinking about someone who died recently. He carried hope around in an old suitcase.'

'You sound stoned yourself now. I know for a fact you have smoked dope.'

'I had enough sense to stop.'

'Mum's right about you. You appropriate all the ... ' she made the inverted commas sign ... 'sensitivity. You leave nothing for us. No wonder Sophie ... ' But she stopped herself.

Now Dad's bass voice filled the room. The others couldn't sing so low.

Laurel leaned, a little embarrassed, against

the mantelpiece, one hip jutting, while he cautiously approached the low G, upright in his tropical suit; still a man that made women use a special bedroom voice.

'Give us an encore, Colonel,' said Dad's brother, the jolly one who always called him Colonel, to remind him of his glory days.

Someone had unearthed some Christmas crackers and passed around the tissue paper hats.

Laurel arranged hers to look like a chic thirties turban and then chose the big golden crown for King Dad.

Bella wore hers like a diadem. Her yellow dress flared into pleats from the sleeves, a fairy princess fallen among earthlings.

Her two boys were sitting on the floor playing 'Guess Who', their rivalry ritualised for the moment.

Norah slipped away into the TV room to check on the fire and found Rufus on his knees going through the documents in Grandma's Saratoga trunk. Just as well she had burnt the journal, Mother's foul-weather friend.

'Someone's been rooting around in here recently. Things are all jumbled up. No one's gone through it since Mum died and we weren't allowed to touch it as kids, remember.' He was brandishing a gilt-edged invitation to Mother's twenty-first birthday.

'Look at this!' Rufus handed her a photograph of her younger self taken by a lover in the South of France. It beamed out a maddening confidence; the unreachable exoticism of foreign parts. What a bitch she had been, crowing over them like that.

'All things passeth.'

'You've bounced back. In love again?' He had been avoiding her. Because she was inconsolable. Tonight she had a new radiance.

Norah knew it was the radiance luck brings. Even the parrots sensed luck in the air. This morning the Rosellas had flown three times around the Juniper tree, like a benediction.

'Here's you and me with Mum at Curl Curl, before we went off to boarding school.' She peered at a tiny fading snapshot. Mother sitting on the grass, Rufus on her knee and there she was, behind them, her arms locked around her mother's neck and Rufus's shoulders, eyes dark with possessiveness. There was the paling fence, the bed of gladioli that always wilted in the salty air. Where was Alex? She must have taken the photo. That must be her shadow on the lawn. What a pain her little sister must have been. Norah felt a surge of that same protective love for Rufus.

'By the way, did Vitek ever come through with the money for your series? Or did I wreck your chances?'

'He's still stalling. It's nothing to do with you. Most of them stall. But I've got a tame doctor, a colleague of Alex, who might come across. We're going ahead anyway. I'm working out the locations, but I'm not sure I can talk my bank manager into a bigger overdraft. I'm not in the mood for a party. I wish we could watch *Brief Encounter*. I wish we could watch it.'

'If Celia Johnson and Trevor Howard were on that train now, they'd be humping away without pulling down the blinds. And the woman who wouldn't stop talking would have her tongue cut out.'

'Anarchy is loosed upon the movies.'

'I remember meeting anarchists in my youth, all with rotten teeth. That's how you could tell they were Libertarians. Too intellectual to go to the dentist. "First we destroy the family, then the church, then the monarchy," they'd intone. And in the process they ruined their teeth.'

'Hmm, they've done rather well, haven't they? You really think video nasties are part of a plot to destroy the family? God, you're paranoid.'

'They're rotting the imaginations of children. First impressions are the deepest. Compare them with what we had – those sweet illustrations in *Wind in the Willows*.

'Bring back censorship, eh?'
'Yes.'

'I knew you'd agree, old thing.'

Justine opened the door holding her drink, swaying a bit.

Rufus handed her a letter. 'This belongs to you. Do you want to keep it?'

'Oh, that,' the girl brushed it away. 'Sophie and I thought for a while we'd be pen-friends. Didn't keep it up of course. We were going to tell all, even what we thought about our horrible parents.' She turned to go. 'You should read it for a laugh. See how the other half live.'

As the mocking girl stood there wedged in the half open door, they caught a glimpse of Dad in the party room, arm in arm with his brother and Justine's husband, taking deep breaths, preparing to embark on *Sweet Adeline*. Laurel was smoothing down the seat of her shantung gown, before placing herself carefully on the window box, her plate of snacks delicately balanced on both knees; soignée to the end.

After a final mischievous wink, Justine went away, and Norah read her daughter's letter:

Hi cos, cos, cos, my pretty little cos, if thou didst know how many fathoms deep I'm not in love.

Boys stink. Only want one thing. But I can give a good imitation of liking it. If I have to.

Know what my Mum's just gone and done? Beat me! Yes, caned me like she was always moaning was done to her at that dreary old school.

Just because I played around with drugs. (You can get a line of smack in the local pub for a fiver.) I've been scoring smack since the lead guitarist offered us his needle, as if it was Mum swanning about with a bottle of bubbly at one of her parties. I'll give it up soon, when I choose to. It won't be a big deal. She's so bloody bossy, thinks she knows it all. Keeps making dark hints about my father not liking it if he but knew. I thought he was supposed to be dead. But she's a bad liar, keeps changing her story. Now he's supposed to be some Polish count or violinist or some bullshit. But she's had so many boyfriends it could be anyone. Maybe someone she met on the ship sailing over here. One of these days I'll turn up on your doorstep and meet Grandad. At least I know he really is my Grandad and cares enough to send me money whenever I ask, which is all the time, tee-hee.

By the way is your Mum still bossing around the restless natives? Seeya, Sophie.

'Probably high when she wrote it,' said Rufus who had been reading over her shoulder. 'What's all this about her Dad? I would have horse-whipped him if I'd been old enough.'

Her brother sat back on his heels and looked at her ruefully. A handsome man still, just a little cadaverous now, time doing its old hatchet job. But Bella in all her ironed glory still had to fend off female predators.

The lid of the Saratoga trunk gaped, ready

to disgorge more oozing Past. Scattered letters shifted in the draught whenever someone came in or out. The curved lid was lined with faded Victorian paper, and it looked wobbly on its hinges. Had she done the damage when she raided it last week and pried open Mother's journal? Now, as if in ghostly retribution, the seamy side of her own life had been exposed.

The trunk had once belonged to her maternal grandmother, an opera singer who performed all over Europe. It was still covered with faded stickers from Paris, Madrid, Rome, even Deauville. Mother had seldom disclosed any information about her own mother except that, in keeping with her era, she had gone in for beating her children; especially after she started to lose her bel canto voice. It was a miracle she hadn't killed their natural love of music.

The door swung open, this time letting in another old uncle, mother's brother, and a snatch of 'Begin the Beguine'.

In the sudden draught, the souvenirs on the floor leaped up and waltzed round the room with the strains of the old song as if they still both held sway in the present.

This particular uncle was Mother's elder brother, the sombre sort, who'd never be seen dead or alive in a party hat. He lowered himself on to the bunk bed. 'Begin the Beguine' was too modern for him. He was waiting for the inevitable Irish medley. He looked at the trunk lying open and gave a bitter smile. It had been in the house when he was a small boy, always locked up.

By now Rufus had come right down to the tissue paper lining. The ancient paper crumbled, revealing a long brown envelope inscribed with faded copperplate writing.

He began to read the documents folded inside which had a galvanic effect on the uncle who tried to heave himself up off the low divan.

Norah gazed on at the flattering photographs of herself. The portrait of the bad grandmother looked down from the wall, her auburn hair coiled on her head; like Queen Mary in a bad mood.

Rufus looked up at his uncle, eyes bright with stupendous news. 'We've got the proof here. One of our great great greats really *was* a convict. She was transported from Ireland for stealing; arrived on the last convict ship, in 1850. After a year she got a ticket-of-leave. We're Aussie aristocrats!'

The uncle jerked back on the bed. 'I knew I should have burnt it,' he moaned.

Rufus put his arms around the old misery whose shocked body wobbled like an old ironing board. He took refuge in his wine, looking cautiously around him. The dado was still fixed reassuringly to the wall, the skirting board lay parallel several yards below.

Music and merriment still wafted in from the piano room. The old family shame had come out brazenly and the world hadn't come to an end. He sighed. Everything was so different now. You could talk about sex in front of ladies. You could expose grisly family secrets. The Present was another country. Sometimes he wished he lived in it.

'Don't worry, Uncle,' cried Norah. 'It's very fashionable these days to have a convict in the family. I wonder what she stole?'

'A bolt of blue cambric,' came the doleful voice. 'She used to live in the west of Ireland. Apparently she'd tell stories about the Arran Islands, which she could see from near their cottage. She used to say that they shone like three silver dollars in the sea. It was the time of the famine. She was young and vain and she wanted a pretty dress. She stole it at the weekly market. Wrecked her life.' He looked at his niece and nephew with malevolence. Hadn't they felt that feckless streak in their blood?

He stood up, balanced on his stick. 'Now they're raking it all up. All the dirty family linen. You both look as pleased as if you'd won the lottery.'

Norah thought of the great great grandma lying in the hold of the filthy ship, pining for the sight of the Arran Islands shining like three silver dollars in the sea, that vision her only legacy.

Rufus shuddered. 'After six months at sea, a pretty Irish girl, I'm surprised she landed here in once piece.'

'Put it back in the box! Put it back in the box! Put it back where Mother hid it!' shouted the uncle, his voice cracking like his mother's when she reached the high C. He was the fourth generation and his teeth were still on edge.

'Come on. It's May I Have the Next Romance With You.' Laurel coiled around the door, her eyes shining like licorice. She wanted the whole world to sing Mother's theme song. But it was she who was having the next romance. She'd been waiting for Dad all her life.

When they joined the party, Dad was absent. Laurel said he'd gone off to get a surprise out of the spare fridge in the shed. Alex was working efficiently through all the tattered song sheets, some from Grandma's time: 'Indian Love Songs', and 'In a Persian Garden', but it was mostly Mother's era, thirties romance, kisses in the dark, trembling moonlight. The candle in the piano candelabra burnt lower in its frilly skirt of red wax. Alex would worry about getting it off the carpet tomorrow. Who had wrenched off its twin? Grandma in a rage? Mother in a tantrum? Or way, way back was it their great, great, great ancestor, in the justifiable fury of the hard-done-by?

The jolly uncle, his party hat askew, whispered, 'Lovely to have you back again, darling. Why don't you stay in Australia? Bring your lovely daughter.'

She gave him a smile. Maybe she would some day, because the things that had drawn her to England in the first place were being eroded. But, well, she had stayed so long over there she had gathered moss.

They were about to begin 'I've Got You Under My Skin' when Dad walked portentously back into the room with a curiously familiar expression – flushed, slightly bloated, with a strong sense of the privilege he was conveying. He laid a bundle of newspapers on the best tablecloth, unwrapping the dry outer layers, then, more cautiously, the wet ones. Inside lay a pile of fresh prawns, weird as creation, still gleaming with the ancient sea shine. He had bought them specially for Norah, she knew it.

Maybe her pride had been stupid all this time, impacted. All she needed to have done was *ask* him for the money. Given him the chance to still be her pa, the provider.

All through the night the mist rose over the gorge. There were no edges to the world. The immense wave came rippling ... rippling towards the house, packing it in wadding.

Bluey had woken in the night screaming 'The mist! The mist!' Norah had rushed into the boys' room, her nightdress billowing. 'He thinks it's really smoke from a bush fire,' explained Bella who had got there first.

But this morning big twists and curls of mist shouldered each other out of sight as the bright pure light opened, a huge eye, in the sky. Chickens were already in a frenzy as the cats stared at them through the wire. Round pearls of dew lay on the flat nasturtium leaves. The grass was blue.

Norah felt like leaping the fence into *Lyrebird* before anyone else woke up. One last search for the mythical bird. If miracles didn't happen, on some days they seemed to come so close. Even the dropped apples in the grass shone as if they were privy to a tremendous secret.

'Wait for me,' said Bluey, running out to the lawn in pyjamas. 'I want to climb the fence too.'

His pyjama legs went flapping off ahead of her. 'Put your feet where mine go.' She was surprised by her lack of alacrity, her caution. That was age. You stood on narrower ground and clung all the tighter.

The woman and the boy jumped on to the grass. A cat deserted the hens and followed them, its eyes glittering. They crept through trees, trying not to break too many dewy spiderwebs until they came to the white rock.

199

'We're sort of trespassing, aren't we?' whispered Bluey.

'Sort of.'

Beneath them the ebb tide of mist had become a streak over the valley where, in the innermost fold, Pete's mushrooms grew. It was still not yet seven in the morning. Her last day was going to be fine.

There was a splashing of big drops on large leaves. And something else. What was it? A faint stirring and shaking, the snap of a twig and then silence, as if someone, something was listening, just out of sight. She waited, silent, hopeful ...

Dad and his brother insisted on driving her to the airport. Although both men were in their eighties, her uncle looked much younger. Lack of responsibility had a slimming effect.

They insisted on taking a detour to Bondi where they led her to the top of the cliff so that she could gaze down on all she was wilfully leaving. The great waves falling into sand, and the kites up above butting against the unending blue.

Then she saw it down by the rocks, a giant sea-horse moulded from sand, all ridged and coiled into its elegant question-mark. So Vitek had been wrong. Sea-horses would never become extinct, at least not in the imagination. They were a necessary magic.

At the airport both old men stood there stubbornly while she checked in and handed over her luggage.

'You certainly travel light, sweetheart,' said her uncle approvingly. But she knew the opposite was true.

Dad peered inside the plastic bag that she would carry as hand-luggage and recognised the parrot on the biscuit tin. 'What have you got in that old biccie tin, dear?'

'Secret treasure.'

She kissed them both, turned away and walked off to have her passport stamped. When she glanced back, they were peering around the barrier at her, their tenacious old faces watching, making sure she was all right, until she moved off, beyond surveillance range.

In the plane she began to calculate her moves: first the bank, then Sotheby's, then the clinic, then the BBC, in that order. All those items in the biscuit tin, whether they were Mansfieldian relics or not, would have to be verified. It could mean a serious biographical documentary, one that would have a more solid foundation than a dalliance with the head of Guy's Dental Hospital. The Genius and the Dentist story still tickled her, but what proof did she have, apart from her own hunches?

As the plane moved over Sydney, over the Blue Mountains and into the desert air she spun herself a new story. The reason she and Pete had been so at ease with each other was that their ancestors had shared the same dreadful convict ship.

She moved her feet to let the adjacent passenger get to the toilets and banged her shin on the biscuit tin. Why hadn't Pete, a man who slept in caves, sold his heirlooms? The answer came to her immediately: he would only do that as a last resort. They were his *Lyrebird*.

For a long time they were flying over nothingness. Just a thick swirling space. She dozed off. In her dream her uncle and her father were trying to reach her through the wall that separates the travellers from those who stay. But they couldn't break through. In a final satisfying flourish they changed into two old dingoes and loped off into the desert ...

SIXTEEN

On the tube from Heathrow Airport into central London Norah noticed a speckled pigeon sitting in a seat on the far side of the coach. It was going to ride all the way back into the fray with her, the little darling.

But soon some brat came along and tried to fondle it. Norah stiffened. Eventually it fluttered out from under his paws and flew all the way down the coach to find sanctuary on the hand rail beside her. But its tormenter came after it.

'Go away,' Norah barked. 'They hate being touched.'

But he came after it once more and the poor bird flattened its feathers against the sliding door as if preparing for the crucifixion.

She snapped at the boy once again. The mother stared at this harridan. But Norah smiled her down, giving orders in her father's brisk voice: 'I'll get off at the next stop. All you have to do is shoo it out into my arms. I'll take it outside and release it into the open air. I've never seen such a strange and lovely pigeon, have you?'

When the train stopped at Hounslow Central, she alighted quickly and braced herself in front of the door, both arms ready to catch the omenic bird. The woman obediently shooed it out of the coach and in the general direction of Norah. But it veered straight up to the top of the indicator and sat there surveying its would-be rescuer with interest.

If it were a smart bird, it might have a chance, providing it found its way through to the escalator and exits. Otherwise it would fly incessantly onward through the dark labyrinth, perched on top of thunderous trains, only to become electrocuted, decapitated, reduced to a smear of blood and feathers.

Norah hurriedly picked up her things and edged back into the train while the doors were sliding closed.

There was only so far you could go to help a bird that would probably shit all over you anyway. It wasn't her daughter, that pigeon, but at least she had got it off the doom train.